KEVIN

vs.

THE CITY OF HEROES

KEVIN

VS.

THE CITY OF HEROES

DEMITRI ALLEN

ARPress
45 Dan Road Suite 5
Canton MA 02021

Hotline: 1(800) 220-7660
Fax: 1(855) 752-6001

Ordering Information:
Quantity sales. Special discounts are available on quantity purchases by corporations, associations, and others. For details, contact the publisher at the address above.

Printed in the United States of America.

ISBN-13:   Paperback   979-8-89389-413-4
            eBook   979-8-89389-414-1

Library of Congress Control Number: 2024919048

CONTENTS

INTRODUCTION

Supervillains. Their kind is a dying species. All the good Supervillains have either died a horrible death at the hands of their own terrifying creations (which end up getting destroyed by a Superhero of some form or another), or they have been arrested and sent to a maximum security prison (Penn. State being the most popular), or they hide away in the cracks of society, too afraid to emerge due to the ever increasing amount of Superheroes.

Villains are meant to be the antithesis of Heroes. They are meant to be the dark force that threatens good, and the Heroes are the light of good that fights back, winning the day in the end.

But sometimes the roles change, with the Hero who loses their way, attempting to change the world for their own ends, and it's the Villain who has to win for the good of everyone else. It's at that point, the Villain becomes the hero, and he/she finds redemption for their misdeeds. It may be a rare occurrence, but it happens from time to time.

Once, there was a great Villain by the name of Baron von Toggelstein. He was a fascist sympathizer who nearly conquered the planet single handedly, under the guise of the one and only Adolf Hitler. He almost achieved the dream of every Villain and Supervillain on this planet, but was cut short by the Allies in the final push for dominance.

Needless to say, the Baron died in the end, and Adolf Hitler was no more. To this day he is heralded the pinnacle of a man who let his vision of perfection corrupt his mind and destroy him completely, a failure in every sense of the word.

Now, I bring up the Baron, and the subject of Villains and Heroes for one reason, and that is because of the man I work for. He is probably one of the greatest Villains of his generation, if not the greatest Supervillain ever.

I guarantee, when his achievements are looked back upon thirty years from now, even sixty years, or maybe even more, he will be seen as the man who proved that you don't have to win to be the greatest there ever was.

Sometimes you just never have to lose.

CHAPTER 1

My name is Shepard, my last name I will withhold for personal reasons. I first came across Kevin upon reading a job offer in the newspaper for a bibliography writer for a villain. Having lost my job at the time, I traveled to the address on the paper, stopping in front of the building shown in the tab.

It was a short building, made of concrete brick painted white. What I thought was strange was that even though it was sandwiched between two much larger apartment complexes, being in the downtown area of Megatropolis, it seemed to stand out more because of its stocky stature. The windows were clear, but covered by closed blinds, and the door was a dark green in contrast.

A handwritten sign hanging on the front door said, "OPEN! Come on in!"

I turned the knob and opened the door to find the room on the other side to be void of most human life. There was a receptionist behind a desk, typing away on the keyboard in front of them. The room had multiple seats, with some plant life to make the room seem more friendly.

The only light in the room came from a single fluorescent light above the reception desk, putting the far corners of the room into darkness.

I walked over to the desk, and waited patiently for the man behind the desk to get finished with what he was doing. While waiting, I observed them, getting to know what they looked like a bit better.

They were caucasian male, with short, cropped black hair, a red shirt, and black cargo pants. He looked to be about eighteen, with his left arm seemingly... deformed. But what really got me were the eyes.

Red. Neon red. They glowed with an intense gaze, as it flickered over the computer screen, his typing quick but staggered, clacking on the keys as he input some garbled nonsense into the document.

It must have been two minutes before he spoke, not stopping what he was doing.

"So, you here for somebody, pal?"

Probably the most informal question for a formal moment. I said to him, "Um, yes. I'm here for Kevin Anderson?"

His eyes narrowed as he looked at me with a begrudging glare. His voice reflected his annoyance, "Have you EVER seen an apostrophe over an 'e' before? It's pronounced An-dray-son, mister...?"

"Shepard. S-h-e-p-a-r-d."

The man leaned back in his chair, and said, "My name is spelled A-n-d-r-é-s-o-n. Suck it, mine's longer than yours!"

A childish grin stretched across his face as he was amused by his bad joke. I quickly changed the subject, "I'm here for the bibliography job, are you still taking applications?"

The mood of the man changed considerably. "Bibliography? Well, shit, if you'd told me sooner, we wouldn't be having a name measuring contest now, would we?"

He laughed and stood up, walking around the desk with heavy footsteps. He walked up to me and grabbed my shoulder with his right hand, dragging me along with a surprising amount of grip for his size. "Well Shep, I hope you know how to defend yourself as well as remember things accurately, since you won't just be idly standing by while me and my gang have all the fun. No sir-ee, you'll be joining us on our quest to conquer the city!"

I stopped cold, just feet from the door he was about to walk through. "Hold up there, Kevin. You mean your whole reason for hiring me is so you can document a suicide mission?"

Kevin slightly turned his head to me, so I could see the half smile he was giving me.

That half smile was one of absolute confidence. The kind of confidence that was almost comforting, that told you that they had it all under control. He said to me, "No, Shep. I hired you so you could document the greatest victory of any one villain, super or not. I'm going to make Megatropolis into MY city. And nobody is going to see it coming."

I nodded nonchalantly, still feeling that somehow this guy had a death wish. But he seemed to know what he was doing, so I didn't question him any further. Kevin dragged me through the door and down a long, dark stairwell.

Though I could see in the dark, it was just barely, since I closed the door behind us out of habit. The thing was, I didn't know what was allowing me to see in the dark at first. It was like some sort of faint glow that surrounded us. After thirty seconds, my eyes had adjusted enough to realize the glow was coming from Kevin's left arm. It was as if he had a glow stick beneath his skin, which to me was kind of unnerving.

After forty seconds, Kevin opened up a second door at the bottom, and light shone all around us. Blinking, adjusting to the light change, I finally saw that we had entered a laboratory of some sort.

Scientists were everywhere, doing something in some way, whether testing some sort of bionic limb or measuring the effects of a dark matte black metal on a plant.

I looked around, observing the activity of the scientists, when Kevin suddenly called out, "Attention, everyone! We have a new ally joining us!"

The scientists paused what they were doing, and all turned to look at their leader. Kevin pulled me to the railing, and said, "This here is Shepard! He's going to be my bibliographer for the big heist! I'm giving him Zealot-level access to our operations, so be aware!"

All the scientists mumbled amongst themselves in confusion. Even I was confused, so I tapped him on the shoulder and asked, "What do you mean by, 'Zealot level?'"

Kevin gave me a look that said, 'Shouldn't you already know?' But, he told me anyway, "Zealot is my second in command. You basically get full access to our plans, nothing held back except the most sensitive of information, like passwords, times, birth certificates and such."

I stood there, slack jawed. I was literally there, talking with him for no more than two minutes, and all of a sudden, he was trusting me with the whole plan? Words could not describe how dumbfounded I was.

Kevin dragged me along yet again, not stopping for anyone. He pulled me over to what seemed to be a control room or an office space, and opened the door leading in. He shoved me in through the door, did a quick once over behind us to make sure nobody was giving us any dirty looks, then slammed the door shut.

Kevin flipped on the light, and walked with his heavy footsteps over to a table that seemed to have some sort of layout for a building all over it. He sat in one of the six chairs encircling it, releasing a huff of air, as if he'd just ran a marathon, or got fired from his job, which was something I could relate to.

He reached with his right arm over to his left shoulder, lifted the shirt sleeve up a bit, and literally pulled the skin off of his left arm. He revealed a mechanical limb replacing what should have been there. He then ran his left hand across his head, roughing up his already roughed up hair even more.

He plopped his mechanical hand on the table and looked at me with the look of a man who had just woken up from his catnap to the smell of wholesome, tasty bacon. I waited, unsure of what to say with the revelation that he was not in fact a whole man.

Kevin broke the silence, "Yeah, I don't have all my limbs attached. I'm like that umm…" he snapped his fingers as he tried to think of the name he wanted. He stopped when it came to him suddenly, "… Seriousman action figure, except batteries aren't included. And I'm missing my left arm, and it's replaced with a three centimeter stainless steel pipe. Not to mention both my legs are springs that don't work for anything except walking and a slightly faster walk."

He pulled his pant leg up enough to show me that he did indeed lack flesh and blood legs. Instead he had what looked like steampunk cybernetic replacements, metal posts with wires, cords, plate metal, joints, and some gears. He put the pant leg back to where it was, and leaned forward, lacing his fingers together with a grim expression on his face.

"I know I'm a freak of nature. I fucking KNOW, I cheated Death more times than that fucking Sisyphus motherfucker who is stuck on a hill and left to roll a huge rock up the fucking thing for fucking eternity."

I was taken aback by the amount of foul language Kevin had to say, but to my dismay, he was just getting worked up. And the cursing just kept coming.

"I've suffered through my fucking life with fucking NOTHING to my name, and lo and behold motherfucker, I finally get the fucking chance to fucking change my fucking life around! Ain't no fucking two bit fucking excuse for a fucked up Villain nor any damned worthless Hero with a death wish gonna get in my fucking way, motherfucker! I'm gonna tear this fucking city a-fucking-part, brick from brick, iron bar from bolt, concrete SLABS from the fucking GROUND!" he slammed his hands on the table for emphasis, "I'm gonna tear it apart, and rebuild the fucking neighborhoods and factories and even the fucking DOWNTOWN in my image—"

It was then, in the middle of Kevin's huge rant, my savior that day came. The door swung open to reveal a man taller than anyone I'd want to anger, with a jacket that seemed to be fashioned from an old high ranking WWII officer's jacket. His pants were long, down to just above his ankles, and a fair tan color. His hair was similar to Kevin's, except it was a stylish look similar to Tom Cruise.

To be honest, he looked a lot like Tom Cruise, if he looked thirty times more serious, and a hundred times more intimidating.

Kevin stopped immediately as soon as that door opened, and when the man walked in, Kevin closed his eyes and gritted his teeth, hissing to him, "Zealot, this better be good."

Zealot glanced at me with a look. The kind of look that tells you that the person who just looked at you, already knows you, knew you were coming, knew you were already there, knows where you live and where you sleep, etc, etc. It was just a very scary look that made me want to panic and run.

But, knowing that my possibility for a paycheck was at risk, I stayed, and moved aside to let Zealot through. Zealot walked up to the table and put his hands on the table, leaning forward to look Kevin in the eye, and he said, "Kevin Andréson, you better calm down this instant, or else I will be required to make you stay behind for the raid on Dark Harbor. I need you to be FOCUSED, and that means managing your rage!"

Kevin clenched his fists for a moment, but knowing his second in command was right, he calmed down and let the tension go from his body. He said in a tired voice, "I'm sorry buddy. This whole plan has been… stressful on me, I had a lot of anger to work out. I finally got that bibliographer I wanted, to document all of this," he pointed at me, with the smile from before that was charming and childish at the same time.

Zealot looked at me again, this time, with a look that said he was okay with having me around, since his boss wanted me there in the first place. I deflated from the stress built up from Kevin's rant, happy that he'd calmed down finally.

Zealot looked back at Kevin, and told him, "The scientists have a new weapon for the heist. I would suggest you and the new bibliographer come check it out. I personally find it rather impressive." He stood up, did an about-face, and left the room.

Kevin grinned at me, seeming to have forgotten the anger episode from sixty seconds ago, and said, "Come along, Shep-my-man. Let's go see one of our new toys!"

Kevin dragged me out of the room, a big grin on his face. I followed along as best I could, trying not to have my arm get ripped off by the quick pace he was keeping. We walked all the way to the other side of the lab, over to a team of four scientists surrounding a strange looking gun.

Kevin went up to them, letting go of my arm, and said aloud, "What's that thing? Looks like some sort of bad attempt at a shotgun."

The scientists all turned to him, and one of them, a brown haired man in a white lab coat and goggles, said to Kevin, "Actually, it's an Amplifier Rifle, but you are close enough, Mr. Andréson."

Kevin laughed aloud and asked, "So what the fuck does it do, Browning?"

Browning waved at the rifle, and stated dramatically, "The CAFDAR Mk2 is an innovation in suppression combat technology, combining lethality and utility in a high power, lightweight anti-personnel assault weapon."

Kevin didn't say anything, he just narrowed his eyes. Browning coughed, "Ah, yes. What it does. Well, the CAFDAR is a semi-automatic rifle, and it has been modified to where whenever it fires a bullet, the round fired is multiplied in the chamber four times over by the Automated Pocket Bullet Module within the weapon. We experimented with the possibility of splitting the bullet up into four quarters, but everything just fell flat. So instead we opted for more bullets rather than complicated division."

Kevin's grin came back, "So I get a four round burst with every pull of the trigger, AND I never run out of ammo?"

Browning nodded, "Yes, that sums it up. It does have a drawback, however. The Module inside WILL overheat if you push it too far, so you need to maintain how many times you pull that trigger in the span of sixty seconds. If you overheat the module, it could irreversibly damage the Module, or even the rifle itself. You need to be careful, okay sir?"

Kevin held up his left hand with the biggest shit eating grin ever, "I solemnly swear, Browning. When do we get to test the sucker out?"

Browning held up his hand, as if telling Kevin to slow down, "When the heist gets underway, then you will all get to test it in the field. We will use the data gathered from your use to see what we can do to improve it."

Kevin pouted, but nodded and said, "Alright Browning, whatever you say. Anyways, thanks for showing us the new gun!"

He grabbed my arm again and dragged me over to Zealot, who was chatting with some other scientists who were doing the testing on the dark metal and the plant I saw earlier.

Kevin said aloud when he was close to them, "Anything new with the Faridian testing?"

The scientists all looked at Kevin, as Zealot moved aside, saying, "It seems that the Faridian is only making you stronger, Kevin."

Kevin's face brightened up considerably, and he said, "Oh really? Nothing but good news today! A major improvement from last week!"

One of the scientists spoke up, "Um, yes, mostly good news. I'm unsure if you'd consider this next bit good news or not, but I figured I would ask…" he coughed into his hand and asked, "So… do you consider having a distinct lack of a soul to be a good thing or a bad thing?"

Kevin scrunched his face in thought, and let go of my poor arm to consider it. He asked idly, "Welllll, what are the benefits and the drawbacks?"

The scientists all looked at each other, silently daring the others to explain it to him.

The brave scientist who spoke before said, "Well, one drawback is that people who say you don't have a soul will be technically correct… one advantage is that any attacks that directly target your soul will be useless. Another drawback is that if you lose the will to live, you will actually die. But as long as you will yourself to live on and keep going, you will continue to do so and heal from any injury sustained. And so it seems, that if you take any damage of a particular type or force, your whole body will adjust to effectively negate any further damage of that type."

Kevin nodded, a thoughtful look on his face, "So, what you are saying, is that if I get shot in the arm once or twice, my body will not only heal the damage, but strengthen itself to keep me from taking that same damage yet again?"

The scientist nodded at him. "Exactly. On top of that, your body gains a natural resistance to ALL damage over time, just from being exposed to Faridian. That's why you've gone from being frail and almost fragile to being almost normal again. The more you are exposed, the more you can take, is effectively what it means."

Kevin's eyes widened, the revelation hitting him. "So, after almost eight years being exposed to Faridian, I'm a million times tougher now? And I'm only going to get tougher?"

The scientists all mumbled their mutual agreement. One of them said, "As a matter of fact, we can replace more of your arm with Faridian parts, just so your body can start adjusting immediately. The raid on Dark Harbor is going to be a big one, and it won't be easy. Probably. Zealot's planning could very well make it a cakewalk if all goes right." He looked at Zealot for confirmation, and received a confirming nod from the man.

After having stood there, taking everything in and listening to everyone, I finally asked the question on my mind, "Kevin, why exactly are we raiding Dark Harbor? Isn't that a military prison and research facility?"

Kevin turned to me in surprise, "Say what mate? You actually can talk? Well I'll be, what a fucking surprise!" He grinned big, and clapped me on the shoulder with his right arm, and told me his goal, sending a shiver down my spine, "Two words, Shepard. Explosives, and Jailbreak."

I immediately began to regret accepting the job. But I knew now, I was in it, and I was in it deep. No walking away from this. I sighed, and said, "Alright. When is the heist going to happen?"

Kevin wiggled his eyebrows, in the most childish manner I'd seen from him thus far. "Tomorrow buddy. We're crashing in, grabbing some explosives, and an evil villain who is the foremost expert in artificial intelligence, explosive munitions, and straight up riot tech, who really doesn't align with anyone whom he thinks will lose."

I honestly didn't expect a fully laid out plan that he was so CONFIDENT in. His assurance was practically palpable, filling me with similar confidence that this could very well work out as planned. I nodded firmly, and he patted me on the back once again, "Alright! You head home and get some good sleep pal. Tomorrow, we're crashing a huge fucking private installation, and increasing our ranks and arsenal! WOO HOOO!!!"

So, doing as he asked, I left the building and went home, and got a good two hours of sleep.

CHAPTER 2

Dark Harbor

I returned to the building the following morning, groggy and hyped up on coffee. Walking down the stairs to the laboratory, I opened the door to find everyone in a mindless buzz, getting everything they needed for the heist gathered together and ready. I scanned the room, looking for my boss.

I found him over by a group of ten men, all getting outfitted with weapons, armor, and other gadgets. He seemed to be giving them a pep talk, getting them all up to date on information they would need. I hopped down the second set of stairs, dumping my empty coffee cup in the trash, and jogged over to Kevin.

When I reached him, however, listening to what he was saying I realized he was only telling them about what he planned on getting to eat AFTER the heist. "Yeah, I was thinking about going to that one Indian restaurant, the place where there's no seats and you have to sit on your knees. Let me tell you, the curry there is nothing to laugh at, holy shit. It's the fucking greatest non-sweet thing I've ever had in my food dish, oh my fucking God."

One of the guys, a guy clad in chainmail armor and sharpening a claymore (two handed longsword), piped up, "What was your favorite sweet thing again, Kev?"

I was surprised that anyone would be informal with the person who signed their paycheck, but Kevin didn't react to the casualty, as a matter of fact he seemed to embrace it. He responded with a dreamy look, "Oh man… Zealot's cheesecake… that shit is like taking a bite out of some lost piece of Heaven! I can't stop eating it, it's so fucking good!"

It was at that point I realized a bit late, that Kevin was nothing like other supervillains I'd heard of. He was just so human, he had likes, loves, dislikes, and hobbies like any of us. What really got me was that he saw himself as unstoppable, unbeatable, at least by what his demeanor told me.

One of the other guys, (this one decked head to toe in heavy ballistic armor) noticed me, and nodded, saying to me, "Hey, you the writer that's supposed to be following us around for the heist?" Kevin turned to look at me, a bit surprised, "Wow, you snuck up on me buddy. I guess Zealot's cheesecake really is my weakness!" He laughed a full, rich laugh, one that made the other guys follow along and laugh with him. I couldn't help but join in, feeling like I was a part of the team already.

We all soon calmed down enough for me to say to them, "Yes, I am the bibliographer who will be joining you. However, given what Kevin has told me, I won't be just a bystander, I will actually be fighting by your guys' side."

All the men nodded at one another, mumbling their agreement to one another. The man who originally spotted me said aloud, "Good, the more guns we have on the field, the better off the whole heist will go. Say, have you ever used a railgun before, writer?" I shook my head, never having actually HEARD of a railgun before. The man however, noticing my blank expression, said to me, "Don't worry, I was just curious as to your actual weapon knowledge. No big deal, as long as you can aim at anyone who isn't one of us!"

The men all laughed, but Kevin remained strangely silent, and was instead staring at me with an intensity I'd only seen before when he was getting angry. I raised my eyebrows in a silent question as to what he was thinking, a question that was left unanswered.

One of the guys, a taller man with standard equipment and wearing a unique helmet from the others (I later found out this was Steve, the squad leader), shoved an assault rifle into my arms, and said, "Here buddy, aim at that bottle over there, and try and shoot it." He pointed at a brown bottle across the room from us, a good thirty or so feet away.

Not really knowing what else to do, I lifted the rifle to my shoulder and took aim. The man immediately adjusted my leg stance using his foot, shifting my legs and feet so that I had stable footing.

Then he adjusted my arms, so that my aim was steady, looking down the sights. He then told me, "Pull the trigger."

I looked to see if the safety was on.

Kevin grabbed the barrel of the gun and diverted my attention to him. He asked, "Shep. Did you just check to see if your safety was on? Because you literally trade safety for lives when you do that."

I was, needless to say, startled out of my wits. But we sat there, staring at each other for long enough that I understood what he was saying. Hesitation was not an option. Action before thought.

Kevin nodded, seemingly reading my mind. He then turned off the safety, and said, "Take the shot Shep."

I aimed, and fired once. The bottle shattered, making a nearby scientist jump in shock. The guys all mumbled agreement, and Kevin smiled. I lowered the rifle, and said to the poor scientist, "I'm so sorry about that!"

Kevin patted me on the back, and said, "Alrighty, guys, get Shep equipped for the raid. Armor, grenades, the works. Make sure our bibliographer gets through his first raid in one piece."

* * * * *

I seriously doubt that I've been more cramped before getting in the van with Kevin's team. The team consisted of about seven people, not including me or Kevin. When including me and Kevin, however, it got really squished in the seats.

Kevin opted for standing in the middle, looking past the front drivers out the front window, talking to Zealot over the radio.

"So, you take squads 2 and 3, and storm the back gates, while me and squad 1 make our way through the East side. With the outer forces distracted, we should have an easy time getting inside. Part of squad 1 will split off and look for 'Professor Blastocyst', while me and Vladmir hunt for the explosive munitions we require for the next raid."

Zealot responded over the radio, asking, "Kevin, what if the kind Professor refuses to work with us for the benefit of our mission?"

Kevin grinned and laughed.

"The guys know how to convince a convict."

Zealot came back and said, "Alright. We're coming up on the gate. Zealot out."

Kevin turned to us, and held his fist in the air, "Get ready boys, we're raiding Dark Harbor!"

All the men in our squad gathered our wits, and when the van slowed to a halt, we opened the back doors and quickly but quietly filed out the back. Kevin came out last, clanking on the ground with his mechanical legs. Kevin twirled his hand in the air, indicating that he wanted us to group up and follow him, then walked over to the wall that separated the outside world. He looked the wall over, reeled back, then punched the wall with his left arm.

Much to my surprise, his fist went right through the wall, just as an explosion erupted from the far end of the compound.

Kev pulled his arm free, backed up, and counted down aloud.

"Threeee… Twooooo…. Oneeeee…"

He snapped his fingers.

The wall where he punched blasted open, the rubble falling all over the street.

I swear, everyone jumped in startled confusion, including myself. Kevin cackled and pumped his fist into the air that he called it. He jumped through the hole, large enough to fit three men at a time, and said to us, "Alright boys! Time to get this shit DONE!"

We all looked at each other, then followed him through, scanning the area for hostile soldiers. Thankfully, the plan seemed to be working, and none were present to set any form of alarm to our presence.

Kevin was looking around as well, however it seemed it was for something else entirely. He saw what he was looking for, and pointed at a big square concrete building, telling us, "Alright boys, that's your quarry. Head in there, find Blastocyst, and get out. Vladdy and I will meet you back here."

The team split and went their separate ways, me following Steve and company. We entered the stockades, on high alert. Everyone scanned for any signs of enemy guards, but it was clear all the way to Blastocyst's cell.

I was impressed with how effective the strategy Kevin employed was. But when we got to Blastocyst, I started having second thoughts.

Gathering around the cell door, Steve opened it with a bullet to the lock, swinging it inward.

Blastocyst was lying on a cot on the floor, seemingly asleep.

He had a pretty sizable beard, but a substantial bald spot on top of his head. His hair showed his age, being grey and shaggy. He wore the gray jumpsuit that all prisoners here wore.

Steve walked up to him and shook him by the shoulder, trying to rouse him.

Blastocyst opened one eye, looking at our leader critically. He then sat up, saying in a generic Russian accent, "None of you are government goons. Who do you work for? Seriousman? Harbiter? K.O.T.H? I would imagine all of them since I've supplied them all with my work."

Steve shook his head and stated, "We aren't here to kill you. We're here to take you to our leader and give you a job offer."

Blastocyst tilted his head, interested. He then stood up and remarked, speaking in his actual English-accented voice, "As long as I get the Hell out of this fucking Stockade, Judas be willing. I was getting tired of the concrete."

We all gathered around him and guided him out of the building, covering all angles we could to make sure he was safe.

We got outside, just as Kevin and Vladimir were jogging over to the stockade, Vlad's backpack loaded with explosives. Kevin threw his arms in the air, a big smile on his face, "GUYS! Did you find the Maddest Bomber?"

Blastocyst pushed some of the other guys out of the way, looking at Kevin directly, "What do you want with me, child?"

Kevin crossed his arms, smiling smugly, "I'm here to give you a job offer. It's pretty simple. You make us some powerful explosives for us, you get pay, benefits, and freedom."

Blastocyst pulled out a pair of reading glasses and put them on his face, scrutinizing Kevin through squinted eyes.

After a moment of staring each other down, Blastocyst asked Kevin, "What reason do I have to trust you over any other person who has recruited me? They all have betrayed me in one form or another."

Kevin looked up, his smile falling.

He seemed… almost like he saw someone he didn't want to see, but when I looked in the direction he did, I saw nothing but the moon glowing overhead.

Kevin eventually returned to his conversation, saying to Blastocyst, "If I was going to make a deal with you only to stab you in the back, you'd know. I make it very obvious when I lie, pal. It's almost a natural reaction to lying, so that I don't do it often. If I DO lie, it's your own God damn fault for believing me."

Blastocyst shrugged, putting away his glasses. "Very well, I really have no other choice, do I? I accept your offer. Get me out of this fucking Stockade."

Kevin waved everyone to the vans, and we all extracted out without a hitch.

CHAPTER 3

The Maddest Bomber

The next few days were spent getting Professor Blastocyst situated in the basement lab, making him his own personal quarters so he could work and live without having to go anywhere.

After we were done, Blastocyst had no shortage of complaining to do, ranging from ranting about the bed placement to having the chemistry station set apart from the containment unit.

But with Zealot being in the room, giving him the eagle eye, Blastocyst was polite about his complaints, and they got fixed quickly.

Eventually the Professor was happy, and thanked us for our patience. I really wanted to interview the Professor, but Zealot shooed everyone out so he could discuss the terms of the deal Kevin made with Blastocyst. I quietly walked around the basement, watching Kevin's scientists do their wacky and complicated experiments. I eventually stopped beside the Faridian testing, watching the scientists expose the plant to mustard gas, only for the plant to continue to be a plant. Meanwhile, a similar plant that wasn't exposed to Faridian shriveled up from being suffocated.

One of the scientists, the one Kevin called Doc at one point (he and Browning were Kevin's head scientists), told me that the Faridian seemed to make it so those who became in tune to its properties had no need for the basics normally required to live in harsh conditions.

They didn't need oxygen, they didn't need to eat or sleep, they could survive radiation levels that would vaporize molecular biology, they had immense resistance to physical damage, and if they couldn't resist the damage, they would heal it so fast it didn't matter anyway. After taking a certain type of damage, to gradually increasing amounts, their internal structures would reform to be able to resist it.

Not to mention, constant exposure to more and more Faridian would force their physical structure to harden and be able to resist literally everything eventually.

Kevin would become… effectively invincible.

Another serious issue was that Faridian was toxic to biological life, if the life in question wasn't already in tune with Faridian, so the scientists who were handling it either needed to use a special suit to transport it, keep it in a thick walled metal box (a minimum of 1 and 1/2 inches was apparently needed), or use machinery to manipulate it.

For this reason, Kevin had a special biofilm to cover his arm to keep from killing people he got near with the Faridian, as well as a secondary steel backup arm in more problematic situations such as an extended meeting.

I scribbled everything he told me down, and I was able to make a list of known laws of Faridian effects.

Law #1: The Literal Rule; What doesn't kill you makes you stronger

Law #2: The Counter Rule; If it isn't Faridian based or Faridian itself, you can weaken, and eventually kill it, with Faridian exposure and wounding.

Law #3: The Rule of Adaptation; If you are already Faridian based, you can become stronger by exposing yourself to more and more Faridian over time.

Law #4: The Sapper's Law; Faridian always extracts energy from any nearby matter, regardless of how much energy is involved.

Law #4, by what I've been told, makes it so the Faridian can't be broken, pierced, or dissolved by anything, except other Faridian samples or for some reason (they got top people working on it), organic material. The only way that it is able to be shaped is with coldfire arc smelting, and even then it takes a lot of time to do it.

The scientists were all taking turns smelting the Faridian into replacement parts for Kevin's mechanical arm, so over time Kevin would be able to expose himself to more and more Faridian, making himself stronger, harder to kill, and overall more powerful.

That and he would always have a deadly weapon on him at all times.

At some point I found myself staring at a small stored sample of Faridian, a piece about the size of a plum. It was a darker shade of black than oil, or coal, or hell even the edge of space. It barely reflected light, which was probably a part of that energy absorption law I brainstormed.

I found myself deeply unsettled by it. It felt almost unnatural. Not in the artificial way, more like in the supernatural way.

As if it was a cursed substance granted to Kevin's scientists by some dark god.

Shaking my head of the foreboding thoughts, I got up and went home. After all, it's not like there would be any cosmic being interested in supplying a deadly yet powerful metal to a Supervillain in order to make him into a god or anything stupid like that. Right?

* * * * *

A few days later, I finally got to have a proper interview with Professor Blastocyst. Kevin stood by the door to the Maddest Bomber's lab/bedroom, as I asked Kevin's new ally a bunch of questions that had been on my mind.

"So, Professor, how did you get caught by the government in the first place?"

"I do not wish to speak about it." He said that as he was soldering a couple of wires together.

"Okay then, would you mind telling us why you got arrested and put in prison?"

"I do not wish to speak of that either, you can look that up yourself."

More questions yielded answers of a similar caliber.

After the fifth question, I looked at Kevin in frustration. Here I was, finally on a good lead, and I'm being blown off by—

"Yo, Professor. How about you stop being a stiff motherfucker and give my friend here the answers he wants, instead of your assholic remarks about not wanting to talk about how you blew up parts of the fuckin city and other parts of the motherfuckin state."

The Professor turned and glared at Kevin. Kevin stood there, arms crossed, his red eyes showing no signs of giving a single damn about the Maddest Bomber. The Professor eventually gave up, and turned back to me, sighing in exasperation, "Fine. What would you like to know first, mister...?"

"Shepard. So... How did you get captured by the military?"

Blastocyst looked at Kevin, then back at me and huffed, "I was taking a leak then one of them knocked me out. Next thing I knew I woke up in the Dark Harbor Stockades, with no way out."

I raised an eyebrow, but I scribbled down what he said. "Alright. Why did you get put in Dark Harbor?"

Blastocyst gritted his teeth and hissed in annoyance, "I'm called the Maddest Bomber, for Christ's sake. WHY DO YOU THINK I GOT PUT IN DARK HARBOR?"

I smirked at him, and replied, "For selling lemonade on the corner that you stole from some poor kids."

Blastocyst probably wanted to strangle me, but Kevin's presence deterred that from happening. I asked next, "So, how did you come across some of your weapon designs? Are they inspired, original, or stolen?"

The Professor nodded and replied, "That's the smartest question thus far. My designs are inspired, mostly, by the weapon prodigy known as Vladorgue Hyperiwan II. He made so many intricate and powerful weapons of war, but sadly nobody paid any attention to his creations except for me. I made some of his most beloved weapons a reality, like the gyrojet projectile launchers and the rotating barreled handguns and rifles. My personal favorites were the ones with reverse recoil, where they got more accurate the more you fired them."

I wrote everything he said down furiously, with Kevin behind me staring at the old man with eyes full of wonder and confusion. He asked Blastocyst, "Gyrojet projectiles? What are those?"

The Professor got a sparkle in his eye. "Think of it as you are shooting little explosions out of your gun, Mister Andréson. They move slowly, but they pack a wallop, especially when you fire lots of them."

Kevin got a glint in his eye, one that inspired wanton destruction. "Can you make one for me, by any chance? It would be the most awesome fucking thing ever."

Blastocyst winked at Kevin, and said, "I can do you one better, Kevin. I can give you a gyrojet rifle, AND an experimental heavy weapon I've been working on."

Kevin started laughing maniacally.

I felt uneasy about these weapons the professor was telling Kevin about, but I decided to keep quiet about it. I asked the next question on my list. "Who have you sold your work to, and why did you decide to sell it to them?"

Blastocyst suddenly turned serious. The really scary kind of serious.

"Are you sure that's information you wish to know?"

Kevin chipped in with, "Um, yes actually. If you gave your weaponry to any crazed villains who intend to blow up, say, the city, we would like to know. More specifically, I would like to know, so I can hunt them down and punch them really hard."

Blastocyst rolled his eyes, and said, "Well, Shepard, Kevin, you know of three of them already. Seriousman, Kingpin of The Highway, and Harbiter. Two others I have sold my work to are Commando Steve, yes, the crazy Vietnam veteran vigilante, and the Overthinker, one of the smarter dumbass Supervillains. And the reasons why boils down to them offering cash and me not wanting to die so I gave them my service."

I wrote down what he said, and Kevin turned outward to shout at Zealot across the safehouse, "YO, Z! We have names on all the new targets we need to deal with! Time to start prep for the next heist, LET'S GO BOYS!"

Kevin clapped his hands together and walked out, leaving me with the professor. I stood up myself and nodded, saying to Blastocyst, "Anyways, thank you for the interview. This will do well in the bibliography I'll be writing for Kevin after this is all done."

Blastocyst looked at me with a humorous smirk, "I have to admit, the lemonade stand joke was a good one, Shepard, even if it was unbelievably annoying at first. Oh, and one more thing…" Blastocyst looked out the door before telling me in a hushed tone, "Kevin is a scary fellow. He seems genuine and carefree, but the aura he gives off is one that says to me, 'piss him off, and he won't hesitate to remove the ribs from your chest'. I am genuinely afraid he will hurt me if I anger him. That's why I'm working with him."

I thought about that for a moment, looking at Kevin as he carried a steel container his size across the room without any help, placing it down for a scientist to rummage through without having to move from his station.

I said to Blastocyst before leaving him to do his work, "Kevin may make you scared, but he won't harm you if you're loyal to him. Just don't betray him, and you'll be fine. That's a guarantee."

Later that night, I thought about what I said, and I will stand by it. Kevin is an honorable guy. Although deep down… I had a sinking feeling he'd show more of his violent side the longer I worked with him.

CHAPTER 4

Prep Time and Video Games

Hello? Hi, is this thing working? Okay good it is, phew. You have no idea how hard it is to type with a big metal fist, so I'm stuck with this stupid speech to text app, but it seems to be accurate. Except when I try to say accurate which is fucking stupid but hey, even modern tech has its flaws. God it sucks with grammar too, it tried to put an apostrophe in "its".

Whoops, sorry, hi, I'm Kevin, the big guy that Shep has been writing about. I really really wanted to put my two sense in on occasion, with my own experiences from my perspective, just so you can, ya know, get an idea on how I think. Hey, it spelled "ya" the way I wanted it to! That's so fucking cool! Sorry, getting off track.

So, the reason why I wanted to hunt down the guys Blasto had sold guns to, is because in order to take over the city we needed to at the very least have superior firepower to everyone else. So by either murdering the possible threats, neutralizing them with diplomacy (that's Zealot's job, I put the parentheses in with my right hand btw), or converting them to our side, we can ensure that we at least have better guns and shit than everyone else.

Some of the targets would be easy to deal with. Overthinker was a coward and a narcissist, so I could scare him shitless OR appeal to his ego, but the former was way more likely to happen than me groveling to get him on my side. He may have moments of brilliance, but it's not worth the hassle. Kingpin of the Highway was a trader, and a businessman at heart. If I gave him a good enough deal, he would stay out of my way and I'd be good to do my work. Commando Steve was a ghost, but a mortal man, so dealing with him was easy. I just had to find him first.

Harbiter was gonna be much tougher, since he was actually a superhuman with a god complex and super speed. He is a fairly on the fence person, neither aligning with good or bad, so trying to reason with him would be a risky play, but ultimately worth it if we can get him on my side.

Seriousman is a whole other ball game.

Soups is EASILY the strongest superhero in Megatropolis, Hell, even the world, some would argue. All of his powers are supposedly infinite, and he's got abilities like flight, heat projection, super strength, super speed, huge durability that makes him seem invincible, and a whole list worth of other powers that I can't even think of right now.

People say he gets all of his powers from the faith of his friends and followers, but my scientists tell me that's bullshit. Seriousman is apparently solar powered, which is a much more powerful and longer lasting source of energy than any faith that the common people can muster in a city like this. If I was going to take him down, I was going to need some strategy to bring down Soups, one that goes beyond just punching him harder. Anyways, that's enough of me rambling about future stuff, let's talk Shepard.

Shep and I have taken some time to know each other, we talked about myself, my hobbies, and my favorite pass times. I also got to know Shep a bit, but he's adamant about keeping that information to himself, since he feels it will "distract from the bibliography", but that's bullcrap. How will people knowing he has a bird distract from my story and my awesomeness? Only if you let it distract the audience! Am I right, or am I wrong?

Of course I'm right, it's storytelling 101.

I like Shep. He's really nervous about being in the middle of this huge fight for domination, but he's rolling with it like a champ. He focuses on getting things recorded and documented, I just do my preparations for the heists coming up.

It's at this moment I'd like to give my little anecdote about the one time Shep found out I played Team Fortress 2.

So there I was, sitting in my office, playing easily one of my favorite games of all time, when Shep comes through the door to my office, giving me that look he always gets whenever there's something going on that he doesn't understand and needs explaining from me.

I paused with a sigh, going AFK next to the other two Snipers and one Scout in spawn, and turned to him, asking, "What is it now, Shep?"

Shepard sat down across from me, notepad out and pen clicked on. "It's about time you told me a bit about yourself, Kevin."

I rolled my eyes and told him, "What else is there to say? I'm a 20 year old guy with mechanical limbs, loves food and violence, wants to conquer the city, and plays video games in his free time."

Shep scribbled that down, and asked, "What videogames do you play?"

I responded with, "Oh, some stuff everyone plays, shooters, RPGs, puzzle games here and there, as well as an idle infinite progression game when I don't want to play anything."

Shep scribbled, then asked, "What are you playing right now?"

I told him, "It's called Team Fortress 2, but it's better known as the war themed hat simulator that took 9 years to develop and 10 more years to improve. The recent update has sparked new life into the old game and I'm really happy with how it's getting to be, though the community is a tough crowd in general."

Shep asked, "The community is pretty crazy, huh?"

I laughed at him, "You haven't seen half the animations these guys make in Source Filmmaker or Garry's Mod. That's shit I can't stop laughing at."

"That's even more insane?"

I waved my hand at Shepard, saying dismissively, "Well, Team Fortress 2 is like, wayyyyy too crazy for you, so, like, for example, you have the Scout, and you put him in a wig, and then he's staring at the sun a bunch, then you have FemScout and you put her in a wig too. And then there's the Spy, and he's the bad guy..."

I paused for a moment to think about what I was going to describe next, "...then FemScout has to die at some point, because... well, fuck that shit. Then Scout's sad. Then he has a sword, and he fights some demons. Then FemScout comes back... she wasn't really dead, because it was actually the Spy. Then Scout and FemScout get in a fight, and Scout kicks FemScout into the sun. Then Scout realizes what he just did and then he's really sad again. Then he's on a bed. Then he looks at a gun. Then he's about to shoot himself, but stops and says, 'Nah, this ain't cool'."

I took a breath, and moved on to the big finisher, "Then he goes, gets on a bike, and he drives off into the sunset, and the sun turns into his mom's head, and his mom's head turns to the camera, and says, 'You done did good kid.' And that's the end of the show, that is EVERY drama TF2 video ever."

Shepard wrote something on his notepad, and then made my day.

"Now all that needs to be done is for you to take that whole speech and render it in a well made animated short film."

That was just one day where he randomly decided to talk to me, and as I found out, he just wanted to get to know me better, to see my motivation for trying to take on the entire Super population of Megatropolis.

It kinda made me happy to see he wasn't going to just be my employee, but actually try to get to see me from my perspective. Hell, the only other person who ever attempted to do that was Zealot, and he soon became my best friend and most trusted advisor because of how well he knew me.

And for those of you with that question in your pretty little heads, yes, I'll tell you about how I met Z later on, when I have time.

As it is we're running down to the wire to get prepared to provoke the Kingpin of the Highway into talking to us. We're gonna hijack a train. Heheheheh.

Hey! The speech to text app can detect laughter! God this thing is so fucking cool!

CHAPTER 5

The Pain Train

Kevin hasn't told me a lot about his second in command. All I know is from little quips from the other men, about Zealot being the most feared and intelligent military leader on the planet, about his strategic prowess and his diplomatic agility. Zealot I did some digging on, and what I found was quite impressive. He alone helped various lowlife factions and small governments in need achieve victory against overwhelming odds, and had spent more than thirty years commanding and conquering with armies ten times smaller than their enemies.

His capabilities as a leader were second to none, but given what Kevin has said to me in passing, he is also the most skilled close quarters fighter on Earth. Kevin had learned everything he could from Zealot, but even that wasn't enough for Kevin to beat his second in command in a straight fight.

I had a feeling, deep in my head, that Zealot had to be far more formidable than he even seemed now, if he is able to fight Kevin to a victory.

And what made me even more nervous is that Zealot was following Kevin and not the other way around. Kevin commanded respect in even a man who was able to beat him. That was actually scary to me.

Coming back on track, the reason I mention my lack of knowledge of Zealot's backstory and current affairs, is that I have no idea how he managed to get a hold of one of the K.O.T.H's locomotive supply trains for this heist.

We were gathered together at the train's stopping point, about twenty miles outside of Megatropolis, in a sandy desert area called the Dunes of the Reich. It was a sizable desert, created artificially during WW2 by Hitler when he launched his first (and only) ICNBM at the States, but missed his target because of a misplaced number. He fired everyone on the missile team after that fiasco (with ovens).

Amazingly the railroad tracks were still intact, which is what the Kingpin used for his nearly untouchable totally-not-illegal trading route.

We had set up tents to keep us out of the sun, but it was still extremely hot out, as Kevin's team set up the train for the explosive surprise they had in store for the Kingpin's second biggest outpost.

Kevin hopped off the train conductor's car at the front, trotting over to me. "Shep, you think you can tell of my adventure on your own, or do you think you'll need my direct input?"

I shrugged, and said to him, "It would be preferred if you told of your experiences that I'm not there for yourself. It would make my life so much easier." He grinned and patted me on the shoulder in a friendly way, "I'll fill in the blanks for you later then, I've been wanting an excuse to use that speech to text program again."

Just then, Doc ran over to us, panting and holding what seemed to be a small pouch in his hand, "Oh thank Archimedes! I caught you in time sir! Here, you'll like this." Doc handed Kevin the pouch, and Kevin blinked at it, confused.

"Doc, what's in this thing? It feels way heavier than I expected."

Doc puffed up his chest in pride, "That there is a highly advanced piece of equipment. It will allow you to pull out an infinite supply of ammo based on what weapon you are holding in your hand!"

Kevin stared at it for a moment. Then he put it on, slipping the belt loop firmly around his waist. He drew his handgun, a .45 caliber weapon, and dropped the clip out of it. He opened the top of the pouch, and sticking out of it was a clip of the exact size ammo he needed. He pulled it out, put it in his gun, then immediately dropped the clip out again. He opened the pouch, just as another clip finished synthesizing out of thin air.

He grinned in that anarchistic way I had become so familiar with, and said aloud, "God fucking dammit Doc, I don't know how ya fucking did this, but I don't care enough to know. I fucking love it, and I'm keeping this son of a bitch."

Doc bowed gracefully, "Enjoy it Kevin, it is sure to help you kill a lot of people."

Kevin gave Doc a high five, and me a fist bump, saying, "Well, Zealot probably has the train ready for me by now. I'm gonna check on him, and we'll see about getting this party started!"

He ran back to the conductor's car, and I looked after him. I asked Doc, "Is he going to be okay?"

Doc laughed and said, "Okay? Kevin's going to have the time of his life!"

* * * * *

Hello? Ah good it's working. For some reason the mic wasn't picking up my voice so I cranked up the registration.

It's me, Kevin, your friendly neighborhood Supervillain. I promised Shep I'd give my input on what happened in this heist, and as annoying as it is to have to talk again to nobody for fifteen minutes only four days after the last time I talked into this mic, I have to grit my teeth and deal with it.

Though, I admit, I still love the app.

So the whole plan was to get the attention of the Kingpin, and the only ways we could do that were A) steal one of his shipments of drugs and crap and do something with it, B) blow up one of his major trafficking buildings out in the Dunes, or C) locate where he did his business and scream at him like a maniac until he decided to listen.

I thought about it, and came to the conclusion: Why not all three in the span of twenty or so minutes?

So I had my ever so resourceful right hand man Zealot organize to capture one of the trains the Kingpin used frequently, and rig it with some of the explosives we got from Dark Harbor. And with that, I was on my way to the second biggest outpost the KOTH had, which was only a half-mile from where the KOTH actually ran his operation.

He would get a huge fireworks display with his coffee.

I was going in alone, half because I volunteered for it, the other half being I was the only one who could survive getting off the train and fighting whatever guards were standing around.

I hung out the right hand side, watching as the complex came into view on the horizon. I hopped back in to put the locomotive into high gear, and the train started picking up speed.

A lot of speed.

This was apparently one of the fastest steam trains ever made, made to be even faster with modern materials and equipment. The furnace was burning white hot, the wheels were chugging faster and faster, and the whistle was actually squealing from the steam buildup. I hung off the side again, the train maybe going 80 miles per hour, and picking up more speed as time went on.

When I was rocketing toward the station at around 100 mph, I pulled the whistle, screaming with excitement, "ALLLLLL ABOARRRRRRRD!"

I then dove off the train, rolling in the sand as the train rocketed at the station, the steel screaming as it careened down the tracks. I stared at it, focusing on the front of the train. Time seemed to slow down as I focused. The train was drawn out to a crawl.

Needless to say, I was startled by the sudden time shift, and snapped out of it.

Snapping back to normal speed, the train crashed into another train in the station, making a wailing screaming crashing sound that was music to my ears.

Then the train exploded.

While yes, we attached about ten pounds of C-4 to the train cars, the cars were fuel tanks filled to the brim with volatile gasoline fumes.

The explosion was glorious, the mushroom cloud rose into the air like a signal. My guys were probably watching this whole thing through binoculars or something. I was not jealous.

I pulled my 8 gauge off my back, pulling the pump.

It was time to get to work.

I started running for the station, the sand slowing me down a bit, but not by much. I saw some guys stumbling around, shocked from the sudden train detonation.

I kept my head down, but when I was fifteen feet from the first victim of mine, I whipped up my shotgun and put a slug into his back. He fell to the ground, the rest of his buddies turning toward the sudden gunshot. I quickly aimed and dropped the both of them, killing them with chest shots.

I reloaded the three shells I was missing from the clip, and continued around the burning building.

The place was basically demolished, if there were any people inside, they wouldn't be coming out, at least any time soon. The flames were bellowing out of the broken windows and walls, probably hotter than they looked, since they were eating a lot of fuel from the trains and building. As a matter of fact, the flames were hot from where I was standing, and I was quite a ways from the building itself.

I eventually saw the small building the KOTH used for his work and business, and the man himself was standing outside, with maybe a dozen guards behind him, all staring at the devastation the train had brought.

KOTH seemed oddly calm for having his building blown up. Actually I'd say he seemed pretty impressed with the work I did.

I figured now would be a good time to approach him passively, so I holstered my shotgun and jogged towards him. One of his guards saw me, then relayed it to the others, and they all got into firing positions in a professional manner, all pointed at me.

KOTH continued to stare at the fiery wreckage.

I stopped close enough so I didn't have to call out that loudly for him to hear me, "So, you like the new renovations? I figured a hellish vibe fit the place better than the industrial one it came with."

KOTH didn't look at me, just stared at the dancing flames as he addressed me, "So, you are the one who did this?"

I gave him a thumbs up, "Hell yeah, nobody else is badass enough to blow up your weapons cache and walk up to your face and literally boast that he's badass enough to jump out of a speeding train just to blow up your shit!"

He looked at me. He waved his hand, and his entire squad opened fire on me.

Now don't get this whole thing wrong. These guys weren't bad shots, and they sure as hell weren't far away enough to warrant missing me. Most of their bullets hit.

They just bounced off of my skin, I was already extremely resistant to ballistic impact. My scientists had taken the liberty of shooting me a bunch way back when, until I could withstand a direct hit from a thermobaric RPG charge. Yeah, that's a thing.

I shrugged my shotgun off my back, brought it up and pointed it at one of the guys. The guy I aimed at, ducked and I ended up shooting his buddy behind him instead. I systematically shot each guy, putting them down with single shots to the head or chest.

When I ran out in my shotgun, I pulled my pistol and killed the rest with the same shots to the heads and chests. Note, every shot they landed (give or take 85% or so, oh my God it put in numbers and the percent symbol yessss) wasn't affecting me at all, and I was wearing a regular shirt and jeans. Yeah, the fabric ripped a little, but my skin wasn't even broken. By the time all the gunmen were dead and KOTH was left standing on his own, I had more holes in my clothes than a house full of termites.

I walked toward KOTH, confident in my stride. He actually looked like he was a bit spooked by my durability, figuring out too late that I was a Super. He asked me, fairly loudly, "Alright, what the fuck do you want? Money? An item I have? What is it you want?"

I stopped and looked at him, glaring sharply into his unnerved face. "Here's what I want, pal. I'm going to take Megatropolis for my own, every square mile of it. I want you to stay out of it, and let me do my work. If I find you're trying to impede my progress, either by directly involving your forces or by supplying someone else I'm trying to eliminate, I WILL hunt your ass down and fucking rip your goddamn jaw from your skull. After I'm done and Megatropolis is mine, I may actually strike a legitimate deal with you, allowing your business to expand to other parts of the global market you can't quite access right now."

He looked around, as if expecting one of his guys to pop out and shoot me right then and there. He looked back to me and asked, rubbing the back of his head in a panic to make a deal and not get shot, "What if I chose to supply you, and aid you in your... crusade?"

I grinned and said, "Well, I'd love to do business! My scientists could use a new coffee maker, and Zealot's been looking at upgrading our arsenal with some more standardized military equipment. Plus, I could do with a better mic and headset for when I'm using the speech to text app to help Shep with his record keeping of this whole operation."

KOTH raised an eyebrow, and asked me hesitantly, "And if I choose to stay neutral?"

I threw my arms into the air, and cried in anguish, "Then we'd have to buy a coffee maker from the STORE!"

* * * * *

So, needless to say, Kevin was very successful in his play to remove the Kingpin of the Highway from the equation. In order to remain in Kevin's good graces, he delivered a new coffee maker, headset, and personalized catalog for Zealot to look through. Kevin and the whole team immediately got to work, preparing to deal with the next target for the move to take the city: Overthinker.

Kevin, a day after the big attack against KOTH, came up to me and asked, "Did you see the explosion after the train crashed? WASN'T IT FUCKING AWESOME?!"

I nodded in agreement, writing on my notepad a rough sketch of a bomb that Blastocyst was building.

Kevin patted me on the shoulder, and said, "Hey, whatcha say you drop by my house tomorrow for some cheesecake and some T.V? I got cable!"

I looked at him, not sure what to say. He clapped his hands together and replied for me, "Deal? Awesome! See you tomorrow!"

He jogged off to his office, his feet clanking on the concrete.

I went back to sketching… only to stand up and run after him.

I had realized I didn't know his address.

CHAPTER 6

Zealot's Cheesecake

Driving to Kevin's place, I honestly didn't know what to expect. Kevin, to me, was an enigma of a person. His motives weren't exactly clear to me, and his erratic and random nature evaded my analytical mind. I just couldn't figure him out for the life of me.

I gathered my thoughts of him thus far, and with what skills I've picked up as a newspaper editor, this is what I have.

He's an angry person. Being around him as much as I have, he tends to explode about various things that make him angry, whether it's politics, the game he's playing, or people being stupid.

Yet at the same time, he rarely doesn't have a smile on his face, loves various things such as food, violence, and internet memes, and never hesitates to give a meta joke or bad pun when he can.

With all this conflicting information, I couldn't imagine what his house would possibly look like.

I eventually arrived at his place, and I pulled up in front of it, parking so I wasn't in the way of the driveway.

I looked out my right side window.

I was genuinely surprised to see he lived in a nice, big house.

It was two stories, white in paint color, with about three windows on the front with a front porch.

I got out of my car, closed it, locked it, and walked up to the front door, knocking hesitantly.

I waited a minute.

I rang the doorbell.

Heavy footsteps sounded from behind the door, and Kevin opened it, a big grin forming on his face at the sight of me.

"Shepard! Welcome to my humble home, come on in!" He stepped aside and I walked in, taking off my shoes and leaving them beside three other pairs by the door.

Upon entering the threshold, I was hit by the most gloriously good smell I've ever smelled.

Kevin closed the door and dragged me to the kitchen, where the powerful smell of grand cooking was emanating from.

I was greeted with the sight of Kevin's monstrous second in command, supremely focused on the oven.

On the stove, he seemed to be preparing four steaks.

Kevin sat down at the island, which seemed to serve as a table for him. Zealot glanced at me, grunted, then returned to his work at the oven.

I sat beside Kevin, and asked him, "So… Zealot has done cooking?"

Kevin laughed at that notion, and told me, "It's Zealot's hobby, if anything. He never gets out of practice, because he does it so often for me and his family."

I looked at Zealot. It was hard for me to imagine the intimidating man to ever have a soft side to him, not soft enough to get married.

It was just then a little girl, seemingly unrelated to Zealot or Kevin in any way, ran up to the tall commander, yelling, "UNCLE UNCLE, ARE YOU MAKING CHEESECAKE AGAIN?!"

Zealot turned to her, smiling the first real smile I've seen from the grim man. He picked her up, and told her, "Yes Hannah, I'm making cheesecake again. I'm also making dinner, so I expect you to finish your steak before you have anything else!"

Hannah pouted, but she replied with "Okayyyyy Uncle Z."

An older woman, seemingly Native American in origin, walked into the kitchen right then, wearing business casual. "Alright Zealot, I expect you to take good care of my baby while I'm at work, and I expect *you*," she pointed at Kevin with a begrudging glare, "to NOT set my house on fire."

Kevin held up his hands, saying "I promise nothing will be set on fire this time ma'am."

The woman nodded, then walked quickly to the front door, slamming the door shut behind her.

I swiveled to Kevin, and asked him, "So, do you live here, are you related to them, or...?"

Kevin turned to me, sighing in exasperation, "Yeah, I live here, but no, I'm not related to anyone. Zealot just lets me stay here because I want to save buying my own house for after taking Megatropolis. It's a security measure if anything, because nobody wants to piss off a man who has more military experience and strategic genius than any general in history, and almost as many connections as there are windows in the entirety of New York city."

I looked at Zealot.

I looked back to Kevin.

Kevin whispered to me, "Zealot is owed by MI6, the D.A.R.K legion, the CIA, and every single mafia known on Earth, those being the Italian, Russian, Amish, and the freakin DUTCH. HE'S GOT DUTCH BROTHERS UNDER HIS THUMB."

I couldn't help but look at him wide eyed. How did Kevin of all people get a person of power like Zealot to work for him? Why wasn't it the other way around?

The questions in my mind remained unanswered, as the food Zealot was making was finally finished. The tall foreboding man dished up all our plates, and passed steaks, mashed potatoes and corn to all of us. Kevin dove in and started eating like a starving dog.

Zealot's niece was taking smaller, more square bites, and I did what she did except with larger cuts. Zealot watched us quietly, not touching his food.

I took a bite, and was instantly sent to heaven.

That steak was cooked just right, tender and juicy, with enough red to be considered rare, but not enough to be undercooked.

The seasoning Zealot had used was beyond my comprehension, yet whatever he had used was amazing.

The sound of happy people eating was the only thing audible for a bit. Zealot noticeably never touched his food. When Kevin was the first one done, Zealot went over to the oven and pulled out a white round cheesecake. He brought it over to the fridge and put it in, covered it with a tinfoil sheet he had prepared, and pulled a second already cooled off cheesecake, then set it on the island, grabbing a butter knife and cutting a quarter slice, giving it to Kevin.

Kevin…. how do I say it?

Devoured that cheesecake with an insatiable hunger I've never seen till then. It was unlike anything I'd expect from a civilized adult, so naturally seeing this behavior shocked me.

Zealot then took the time to eat his food.

By the time Kevin was done eating, me and Zealot's niece had grabbed our own slices.

Kevin leaned back, smiling smugly. Zealot's niece started eating hers, and I eyed a small bite of my own.

I'm not a cheesecake fan, normally. But, given how good Zealot's other foods were, I said why not, and took the bite.

My field of view widened, and I dropped the fork.

The taste was…. indescribable.

In a good way.

There was no hugging myself, no floating in the air, I was just in another state of nirvana.

I understood why Kevin's weakness was Zealot's cheesecake, with that one bite. I came back to reality when I felt cold water splash my face.

Blinking, I wiped the water out of my eyes and stared at Kevin's water glass hovering in front of my face.

Kevin tapped the back of my head, "Shep, you okay? Command to Shepard, please state your current status."

I looked at him, and said nothing. I think the look in my eyes said it all to him. He gently slid the plate of cheesecake away from me, saying to Zealot, "I think he's had enough for one day. Any more and he might go into a coma."

I lay my head on the table, trying to reboot my brain from that experience. Kevin finished my cheesecake slice as Zealot finished his food and nabbed his own slice of cheesecake.

After a few minutes of staring at the dark and still sort of warm marble countertop, I eventually sat back up to find that everyone else had moved to another room. Standing, I headed into what I assumed to be the living room, where the sound of news anchors came from.

I peeked around the corner, and I think I had a second stroke then, because my jaw almost smashed through the floor.

Zealot's TV was massive.

It was theater sized, covering most of the wall, somewhere in the ballpark of 100 to 125 inches.

The two men's eyes were glued to the broadcast as Zealot's niece played on a tablet.

I focused on the news anchor.

"... and the mayor claims that Seriousman is in consistent contact with him, informing him on the development of the other villains' movements. Seriousman promises that by the end of the month, all villains in the city will be brought to justice. He is always on watch, and hunting for evil within our city's streets—"

Kevin muted the television, and stood up, looking at Zealot. "We have to get going. If Seriousman is on the move like this, that means he's planning something, something we don't know of. If he says he'll bring 'all villains to justice', then he's probably going to put whatever he got from Blastocyst to use. We need to do the heist against Overthinker as soon as fucking—" he stopped, and cleared his throat, seemingly not intending to curse, "— as soon as humanly possible."

Zealot immediately pulled out a phone and sent a message to someone, and said to Kevin, "Scientists are getting everything ready now, Kevin."

Kev smiled, and looked at me, seeming almost glad to see me, "SHEP! I was beginning to think you'd never get up!"

* * * * *

When I went home that night, I fed my bird, and lay on the couch, stared at the ceiling a bit, I couldn't help but think about what Kevin could have been worried about.

Yes, Seriousman was a threat to him, mostly because of how much power and influence he had. But Seriousman promising to get rid of villains all across the city wasn't anything new.

I wondered what about this time made his declaration of war on evil any different from previous times. I eventually passed out, thoughts of cheesecake and explosions filling my head.

CHAPTER 7

Can't be Thinking THAT Hard

Walking into the basement level the next day, more coffee in my hand, the place was indistinguishably busy from the first day for the raid on Dark Harbor.

The big difference was in the atmosphere.

The people moving about were dead silent, only exchanging brief words of needed info and critical supplies. Even the soldiers at the end of the room were unusually quiet, all cleaning weapons and fitting body armor. I quickly went down the steps, and walked over to the soldiers, tossing my empty coffee cup in the trash. I asked the guys when I got to them, "Hey guys, what's going on? Why is everyone quiet?"

The men all looked at each other, then at me. One of them, a squad leader called George, said to me quietly, "Kevin came in, and he was furious. Zealot tried to calm him down, but Kevin just stormed off into his office. Zealot called a 'Code Temperance', to work as quietly as possible in order to keep from disturbing Kevin."

I looked at them each, and each in turn nodded in agreement.

With a shrug, I said, "Alright then, I'll go see what's bothering him."

I turned and started walking for Kev's office, ignoring the hissing and nervous whispers of the soldiers behind me. I went up to the door, and gave a firm knock.

A minute passed.

I knocked again.

Kevin answered a moment later, saying in annoyance, "Who the fuck is knocking—"

Upon seeing me, he stopped himself, clearing his throat. "OH, Shep. Hey dude. Come on in, have a seat."

I walked in at his bequest and shut the door behind me. He thumped his way over to his desk and sat down in his chair. He looked at me with an exhausted smile, and asked, "So, whatcha need buddy? Something bothering you?"

I shook my head, and said to him, "No, I was about to ask you that exact question, Kevin."

Kev sighed, seemingly deflating like an angry man shaped balloon.

"Yeah, yeah, it's just… Blastocyst called me the other day and… told me what Seriousman had. It's bad news and good news, but it honestly worried me so much it kept me thinking about it all night. The good news is, we may have more time than I thought we did, since he hasn't completed building it. The bad news…" Kevin chewed on his thoughts before finishing his sentence, "… well, if he finishes building it and gets the thing to work, there won't be enough of us to take over Megatropolis. Hell, there won't be enough Megatropolis to take over."

I tilted my head at him. "So, I take it you got no sleep last night? Is that why you're cranky today?"

He laughed and shook his head, "No no no, that's not it. I don't NEED sleep Shepard. The Faridian adaptation I went through completely nullified most of all my human limitations, including a need for food, water, air, and rest. While yes, it is still beneficial for me to do all those things from time to time, I don't need to do them at all. The thing that's bothering me is… well… what if we don't pull through in time? What if we fail to beat Seriousman? What happens then?"

I was truly taken aback. Kevin Andréson, the great and powerful Supervillain, the unbeatable and unbreakable powerhouse, was having doubts about whether or not he could beat Seriousman in time. I took a bit of time to think about what to say. I eventually said this:

"Kevin, we've known each other for little more than a handful of days. I have seen you take risks that no other human being, whether Super or not, would have ever dared consider. We raided a secure government compound without anyone even knowing we were there, I watched you jump out of a speeding train, albeit at a distance, and I've spent enough time getting to know you and your personality, that I honestly, truly think you can do it. You aren't a hero, nobody here denies that. But just because you're a villain, doesn't mean the heroes are going to win against you. You're skilled, tough, bold, brave, trigger happy, violent, confident, and moreover, a badass. I have no doubt in my mind you'll pull this off, and take the city for your own. Build the downtown in your image, am I right?"

Kevin looked at his desk. After a moment, he finally looked back up at me with a smile on his face, and said, "Thanks Shep. I feel much better now. Let's go fuck up Overthinker's day, eh?"

I nodded at him, "Let's go boil this guy like the chicken he is."

Kevin laughed uproariously, slapping the desk and standing up, "HahaHA! Awesome, Shep! I ought to give you a pay raise just for that quip! I'm stealing it now!"

He jogged past me, pushing open the door and yelling across the warehouse, "BLASTO! WHERE'S THE SHOTGUN YOU PROMISED ME?"

* * * * *

I dove behind a concrete barrier, a hail of bullets flying over my head. I covered my ears as the automated turret unloaded a huge number of rounds into the stone. I had to ask myself how I got there at that moment, and whether or not I would be able to leave alive.

Just as I feared I was done for, the familiar sound of metal pounding into concrete broke through the noise of gunfire.

Kevin skidded into view around the corner, an assault rifle in his hands. He ran directly at the turret, seemingly unaffected by any of the bullets that hit him. I didn't see what he did to the turret, but the sound of tearing metal and gunfire let me know he broke it and moved on to the next fight.

I stood up slowly, peeking over the barrier.

The turret was gone.

Not broken and in pieces, it was just gone from the stand it was on.

The only conclusion I could come to was that Kevin ripped it from its base and was now using it to cause all kinds of trouble for Overthinker's robots.

Wait, you're lacking context.

So Overthinker's headquarters lies beyond city limits, in an underground bunker he built himself with the money he receives from his technically legal coffee chain he manages in the city.

Turns out Starbucks wasn't the one who had a monopoly on coffee in Megatropolis.

In his bunker he's spent the last year and a half building an army of heavily armored and armed warbots, probably to try and take over the city with what amounted to a blitzkrieg.

When we busted into the bunker, we were met with a large defensive force, armed with conventional weapons and explosives.

Kevin gave Zealot his coffee, told everyone to stand back, and dove into the fray.

While the first responding force was busy trying to fend off a destruction-happy Kevin, me and Kevin's elite team (Steve's group), made our way around the edge of the upper level, avoiding conflict where possible and heading for the stairwell down into the compound.

Along the way, we ran into a force of bots, and while the others retreated through the door we came in, I stupidly ducked behind the barrier instead of following them.

You know what they say, hindsight is 20/20.

And now I was following a path of absolute devastation, wrought by my employer in his adrenaline rush. The team eventually caught up to me, and we all followed Kevin's trail, marked by pieces and scrap and mechanical corpses.

We went for a solid three minutes without contact with any functional machines, heading deeper into the bunker, where there were fewer, but visibly more advanced machines.

Upon closer observation of one of the fourth floor bots, we found that some of them had Professor Blastocyst's specially made weaponry, the "Gyrojet" projectile weapons he had supplied Kevin earlier.

Had Kevin not received the ones he did earlier that day, he probably would have confiscated at least one or two of these for his own use.

The last floor of the bunker was floor 6, but we had to access this floor via the stairs, because the elevator we would have taken was broken open and the wire was snapped.

More stairs, more corner checking.

We went through the door, and entered into what was a huge construction warehouse.

A warehouse for constructing gigantic mechs.

Well.

It probably did at some point.

Being as far behind Kevin as we were, he had plenty of time to not only fight and destroy four separate mechs on his own, he also broke the equipment and machinery used to make the titanic machines.

While Kevin would get an earful from Zealot about wasting the construction bots later, at that moment me and the squad were dumbfounded by how powerful Kevin was when he was on a destructive rampage like this.

We advanced, carefully maneuvering around the obliterated mechs, until we came to a door where Kevin sat on top of another robot, eating a sandwich for God knows what reason.

He waved at us as we walked up to him, and he said, "Took you guys long enough! I had all the fun without you! I figured I would wait up for yall so you could see me scare the living hell out of Overthinker."

Steve saluted Kevin, stating, "Sir, the compound is secure now. Although we sort of wish you left some robots for us to break, sir!"

Kevin waved him down, saying in an exasperated tone, "Whoa whoa whoa, calm down with the official language Steevy buddy! I hired you for your skills and experience, not to be called 'sir' or whatever! I'm not the President of the United States! At least not yet..."

He chuckled to himself like only he knew what would come in the second book.

Steve coughed and said, "Sorry Kevin. We're going in to beat this guy up or...?"

Without another word, Kevin stood up, turned around, reeling his mechanical arm back, and he punched the metal door.

The door itself bent a bit from the impact, tanking the heavy left swing from my employer.

The concrete around the door didn't fare as well.

With the screaming sound of iron reinforcing bars being torn in the midst of solid concrete breaking from intense impact forces, the section of door and wall fell to the floor, slamming down hard.

In the room beyond, the Overthinker stood, alone, staring in utter terror at Kevin, who laughed aloud, entertained by the fact he punched a door and its frame out of the wall.

Kevin walked on top of the door, approaching the self-proclaimed mastermind as we all filed in behind Kevin, surrounding the Overthinker with our guns raised.

Kevin stood in front of the scared man, looking him right in the eye. They stood like that, eye to eye, for a terrifying thirty seconds.

The Overthinker shrieked after those thirty seconds, after he stuttered "WHO ARE YOU AND WHAT DO YOU W-W-WANT?!"

Kevin didn't reply.

He just smiled, showing his teeth.

A shadow fell over his face as he did, one that hid the top half of his face, so only his glowing red eyes and his sinister grin showed.

The Overthinker was scared out of his mind.

The scientist curled up in a fetal position right then and there, blubbering and sobbing like he'd just been surrounded by a mob of angry bears.

The only thing was, we as a squad weren't what scared him.

It was the Supervillain standing over him at that moment.

Kevin reached over the scared man, and pressed a button on the wall that said "emergency shutdown".

A vox voice echoed through the bunker, "Bunker defenses, deactivated. Rerouting power to repair and reconstruction."

Kevin turned around and walked away, leaving Overthinker on the ground. The man looked up cautiously, hearing Kevin's clanking feet moving away from him.

As quickly as he could, he got to his feet, and with shaky hands drew a weapon from his belt.

Steve called at him, "OVERTHINKER, DROP YOUR WEAPON NOW!"

I didn't even see Kevin move.

Suddenly, Overthinker screamed in agony, his hand twisted and crushed in Kevin's mechanical grip.

Kevin's face was completely in shadow this time, his eyes closed.

"You want to know what I despise about humanity, Overthinker? What I absolutely cannot STAND about human nature?"

Overthinker couldn't respond, he just uselessly and weakly grabbed at Kevin's hand with his free hand, trying to get his broken hand free.

Kevin told Overthinker his thoughts.

"COWARDICE. I hate the fact that it's in our nature to be cowards. To fear the dark. To fear animals. To fear what can hurt us. To fear anything we decide should be feared."

Kevin's head tilted, as Overthinker bawled from the pain.

"I especially hate it when humans use fear as an excuse to be underhanded jackasses, trying to get the upper hand by stabbing someone in the back, or by surprising the enemy during a time meant to celebrate peace or prosperity. True people face their fear head on. True humans will fight their enemies face to face, or use tactics that don't involve cowardice."

Kevin let go of Overthinker's hand.

The poor man clutched his hand, sobbing uncontrollably.

Then, Kevin grabbed the man's head between his hands, making the Overthinker look him in the eye.

"I hate you, Overthinker. Oliver. Oswald. Whatever your fucking preference is. You are a coward. You are not a real Villain. You are a joke, hiding behind a wall of machines because you refuse to develop social skills and HIRE REAL PEOPLE."

The Overthinker was stunned into silence. Then he resumed crying, making me realize that Kevin wasn't actually intimidating him.

Kevin was trying to get the man to become a real part of society for once, instead of trying to fight society.

The broken, scarred man stuttered through his sobs, "I-I-I'm s-sorry— *sob*— I-I am a— *sniff*— c-coward. I-I want to-to t-take— *sob*— take it a-ah-all back. I w-w-want to st-stop this. Puh-ple-please... don't kill m-me..."

Kevin's face returned to form, setting into grim acceptance.

"Okay. I believe in second chances. You seem to have learned your lesson. Stop playing the Villain, make some real friends. You make good coffee, use that to your advantage. Stop building armies, and start building a life."

That seemed to bring the Overthinker to his senses. He did what little nod he could, given Kevin was gripping his face.

Kevin let him go, and waved us all to follow him.

Overthinker was left there, clutching his shattered hand, with a new lease on life.

* * * * *

The bunker was secured completely by the end of the day. Overthinker, aka Richard Taylor Wesker, was escorted home by a small team of Kevin's soldiers, and we had access to all of his weapons and supplies within the bunker.

That alone would give the crusade a huge leg up in firepower if ever it were needed.

I found Kevin looking through the Bunker's computer, the young man seemingly focused on finding something. I went up and said to him, curious, "So, what's up Kev?"

Kev turned to me, startled out of his trance, then smiled his usual big grin at me, "Shep-my-man! I'm just checking to see if a particularly important something is here. I have a feeling though, I'm not going to find it."

I looked at the screen, then back to him.

"Okay then. So, I'm assuming Commando Steve is our next target?"

Kevin waved that off, saying dismissively, "Nah, he's one of those guys you have to react to when he shows up. The real next target is Harbiter."

My heart sank when he said that.

Harbiter was a very powerful Superhero, one who was super fast and extremely unhinged. Some say he could outrun light speed, and his power allowed him to generate so much electricity he could fire lightning from his hands.

He was also a Hannibal fan.

It led me to thinking about how fast Kevin was. "Kevin, how were you able to move so fast earlier?"

Kevin turned to look at a wall, thinking about it. He turned back to me, and said, "If you are talking about when I was tearing through the bunker, I normally move that fast. If you are talking about when I broke Overthinker's hand, I really don't know. The best I can describe it is that I think so fast that time slows down for me, so I'm able to react quicker. The only thing is I don't know how, and I can't really control it. So, I'm going to ask Doc or Browning about it tomorrow, see if it can be utilized in the future."

I blinked at him, but accepted his answer. He genuinely seemed like he had no idea what it was that made him so fast, despite having 50 or 60 pound metal limbs that should impede his speed significantly.

He would have to overcome physics themselves to be able to move faster than the eye could detect. But it seemed that it just might be the case.

We would see what it was, come tomorrow morning.

CHAPTER 8

FOCUS Testing

The morning after raiding Overthinker's bunker I came down the stairs to a more normal day at the office. Sipping my coffee, I looked around the basement lab to see scientists working and doing their research, and the soldiers and smiths maintaining their equipment.

Surprisingly I saw Overthinker in a far corner of the room, talking to Zealot.

I looked around for Kevin. He had sat down with Doc and Browning, explaining something to them. I jogged down the rest of the stairs, tossed my empty coffee cup in the trash, and went over to the trio.

As I came within earshot, I heard Kevin talking about his confusion with his sudden bursts of speed.

"So the first time this strange 'focus' speed up thing happened was one time when I was reading a really good book, I can't quite remember what it was. I was sitting there, it was 3:00 PM on a Thursday, I was on chapter 3 I think. I got to this really gripping scene and I was riveted, to the point where I brought the book in closer, as if I could get closer to the action. I read through the whole novel, all 300 pages or so, in just that day alone. When I finished the book, I closed it and set it aside, letting myself recover from that awesome read, and naturally I looked at the clock to see how long it took me..."

He trailed off and stared at the Faridian sample in the protective plexiglass box, seemingly trying to recall what he saw on the clock.

"...... It was 3:01 PM. I read the whole fucking thing, from the third chapter to the last page in the span of SIXTY SECONDS."

He looked at his head scientists, Browning had taken notes and was sharing them with Doc, the both of them trying to grasp what Kev was telling them.

"The second time it happened when I dropped a fragile set of china that Zealot's sister owned. I almost went into a panic trying to catch it when I realized it wasn't falling that fast. It was barely moving at all. I grabbed the set of cups midair before they could hit the ground, and when I did that time returned to normal."

More notes from Browning. More quiet discussion I could not hear.

"The third time happened when I watched the train approach the KOTH's station, and I stared at the front, trying to absorb every detail. I was shocked out of it when I realized time was slowing down."

Browning and Doc put down the clipboard and looked at him with concern as he finished with his last anecdote.

"The most recent time was when Overthinker drew a gun on me. I heard Steevy yell at him, and suddenly I heard all the noise fade away until there was only silence. I turned around and saw everything was frozen in time. It was like I had stopped it or something. I was still mad at Overthinker for being a coward so I went up and squeezed my mechanical hand around his wrist. My gripping met no resistance. I'm pretty sure I pulverized his bones. I tried unfocusing, and that seemed to pull time back into normal movement."

He frowned at the two men, "Guys, do I have a secret superpower I never knew I had, or is this a result of the Faridian? And how in the fuck am I supposed to control this power normally?"

The two scientists looked at each other and seemed to nonverbally communicate with their eyebrows and shoulder movements.

Then they turned back to Kevin, and Doc said, "I have an idea Kevin. One second." Doc got up and ran to his desk by the back wall, grabbing a Rubix cube and waving at Kevin to stand up. When Kevin did, Doc shuffled it into a simple pattern, held the cube up in his hand, and told Kev, "Alright Kevin. Focus on the cube. When I say so, I want you to solve the cube."

Kevin raised his eyebrow. "Doc, how am I going to solve it..?"

Doc suddenly threw it at Kevin.

Kevin seemed to momentarily hold up his hands to catch the cube, but he blurred and then suddenly was standing beside Doc, leaning on his shoulder with a completed Rubix cube on top of the scientist's head.

Doc stumbled, the cube dropping on the floor.

Kev smiled and looked around the basement. Following his gaze, everyone was confused because NOBODY WAS WHERE THEY ORIGINALLY WERE. The soldiers were all in random places around the basement, the scientists were all in a group in the corner where the soldiers normally would be, Zealot and Overthinker walked out of Kevin's office, both really confused as to how they got there.

At least, I assumed Zealot was confused. Overthinker certainly seemed so.

The only thing I was wondering was, why wasn't I moved?

Then I realized my wallet was gone.

Kevin looked at me, tossed my wallet to me, and suddenly was in front of me, *handing* me my wallet.

I was so confused, and I just slipped it back into my pocket.

Kevin walked over to Doc and Browning, and threw his hands into the air in victory, "I figured it out! All I have to do is FOCUS! And suddenly I speed up so fast, time is like it stopped!"

Browning gave him a thumbs up, and Doc smiled, picking up his cube and heading to his desk.

Discreetly as possible I went over to Doc, tapping on his shoulder as he placed the cube on the desk. He turned to me, a bit surprised to see me. "Shepard! How can I help you?"

I looked around really quick, and mumbled to him, "Doc, what's going on with Kevin? What is this ability he has?"

Doc frowned, "Well, it's something I think he got from the Faridian adjustment process. It seems he can focus his brain function and efficiently accelerate his thoughts to unheard of levels. He can perceive things much much faster than a mortal man. I think… possibly even beyond superhuman."

I thought about that for a moment, and hesitantly asked, "How… fast can he go *exactly*?"

Doc paused.

He looked at Kevin with a mix of fear and… intrigue?

"I don't think there is a limit to his speed. In theory… no, it's entirely possible for him to move so fast that… time itself will have trouble trying to keep up with him."

I am not a genius when it comes to physics but I had to ask something else about Kev. "Why doesn't his body rip itself apart when he moves? Moreover why didn't we all die when he touched us and moved us?"

Doc shrugged, "I doubt he was moving fast enough to kill any of us by moving our bodies out of our original positions. As for him, I have a theory that the Faridian adaptation actually made his native internal structures inherently linked subatomically. His body is tied at a quantum level, unable to be separated by equivalent forces. While yes, at a macro level his body can be damaged, he is effectively immune to being atomized or ripped apart from gravitational forces or kinetic forces."

I put my hand to my forehead.

"So what CAN'T Faridian do for him?"

Doc looked at me and smiled.

"Faridian can't make him anymore human."

He patted me on the shoulder and walked off.

* * * * *

The next day I was driving to work, I felt light and ready for the day. I felt so good, I didn't even pick up my morning coffee that day. I had got some really good rest and even better I had breakfast.

I felt great.

Turning the corner onto the road where homebase was, I saw smoke in the distance.

Oh God.

I put my foot to the floor and got there as fast as I could.

I pulled to the curb, and got out of my car, slamming the door shut and running to the other side of the road where most of Kevin's men were gathered, scientists and soldiers working in tandem to help the injured.

The building was billowing out smoke.

I ran up to Steve, and got his attention as he surveyed the bustling men, "Steve, is everyone okay? Did everyone get out?"

Steve looked at me with a blank expression, a stoic one that was uncanny for him.

"Almost everyone got out, only one is unaccounted for. Professor Blastocyst is nowhere to be found."

A sinking feeling in my chest.

Dread.

I had no idea what had come over me, but I felt like I needed to go and save the Professor. I pushed past Steve and ran for the building, the soldier breaking his stoic facade to call after me, telling me to come back.

I ignored him and held my breath, diving into the smoke and heading for the stairs to the basement.

I quickly ran down the steps, stumbling into the blazing basement lab.

I exhaled, and covered my mouth, breathing shallowly through my jacket. I went down the final set of steps, and remembering high school fire safety training I ducked down low to avoid the rising heat as best I could.

I crouch walked my way to Blastocyst's room in the back, pushing open the door ajar and calling out for him.

"Professor! Are you okay?"

I looked around, and spotted him beside a small vault, propping against it and facing the door.

He smiled an almost relieved smile at me, saying to me, "Shepard… good… I wanted to… tell you a few things… before I died…"

I shook my head and hobbled over to him, "No Professor, I'm getting you out—"

"Like Hell you are boy, now listen! Harbiter was the one who attacked the lab. He intended on getting rid of Kevin and Zealot, but they had gone home, so he torched the whole lab! He had no idea I was here, and I don't intend on anyone ever learning of me escaping from prison."

I hesitated, looking at him critically.

"Professor, you aren't saying…?"

"Yes, Shepard. I intend on dying here. And I also intend on making sure none of my work gets into any more hands than it has already. Seriousman may be making my ultimate weapon, but even he doesn't know the flaw in my design. I made it easy to disarm."

I shook his shoulders vigorously, "Blastocyst! What are you talking about?!"

He suddenly gripped my shirt and pulled my ear to his mouth, and he said into it, "Tell Kevin, if Seriousman finishes building the bomb, that if he cuts the power, it will shut the bomb off and prevent it from detonating."

He pushed me away and opened the vault, pulling out a small football sized object and twisting one end of it.

The bomb he was making before.

"You got two minutes Shepard. Get out of the building."

My eyes widened and I shot up, running for the exit. I forgot all about fire safety for the moment, and I felt the searing pain of the roaring chemical fire against my skin and jacket as I ran through the lab, then up the stairs as fast I could. I dashed for the exit door and dove out, rolling on the ground as if I was doing parkour.

I came to a stop beside some of the scientists, coughing and sputtering the smoke out of my lungs. Thankfully I managed to inhale very little so I calmed down in seconds.

A few seconds after that, the bomb went off.

With the sound of thunder and pure energy, the ground beneath us all shook and rumbled, and the building we called home crumbled, falling in on itself and disappearing from view, leaving a crater where a small, stout, and proud building once stood.

We all stared for a long time, until the sound of clanking metal broke through the silence.

Kevin "Motherfucking" Andréson, our leader and the angriest man alive, walked over to the huddled men with a look of pure outrage on his face.

He glared around, and yelled at the gathering, "WHO THE FUCK DID THIS? WHO BROKE OUR FUCKING BUILDING? WHO'S SPINE NEEDS A FUCKING REMOVAL OPERATION?!"

I walked over to him, the sight of me causing him to simmer down. I put my hand on his shoulder, and I said to him, "According to the recent Professor, Harbiter was the one who attacked us, Kevin. And the reason why the building is gone… well, Blastocyst didn't want anyone else to find his work."

Kevin looked at me with a stare of disbelief. He looked at the crater. "He's… dead? God fucking damn…"

I patted his shoulder, and brought him in for a bro hug.

Kevin took a moment, but he hugged me back. After a few moments, he let go and addressed the rest of the group, "Is anyone else missing or seriously injured?"

Browning raised his hand, kneeling over by Doc, who was covering his left eye with his hands, "Doc got shrapnel in his eye, he's going to need real medical attention, and soon."

Kevin pointed at Browning and stated, "That's covered in your insurance plan with me, get him an ambulance and on his way."

Browning nodded and pulled out his phone dialing 911.

Kevin looked around for any other hands, but when no one stepped forward, he nodded and said, "Alright people, gather together and pack into the vans. Our new base of operations is being moved to Overthinker's former base, now that we've commandeered it. It will be easier to defend anyways, what with the mile or so of desert around us."

And with that, everyone got up and moved to the vans, the thirty or so employed piling into the back of all three large transport vans.

Kevin turned back to me, giving me a solemn but hopeful thumbs up, "Okay buddy, you head home for today. We need to get set back up at the bunker anyways, and you could do with the extra rest and spend some time with your bird. What was their name?"

I kind of looked aside at Browning and Doc, seeing the two hugging each other, almost like best friends. I said to Kevin, offhand in a way, "His name is Stu. He's a good bird. Polite. Doesn't eat much, nor does he talk too much. Good bird."

Kevin smiled at me. "He a gud birb?"

I agreed, "He a gud birb."

He chuckled and patted me on the shoulder, "Go home Shep-my-man. I'll call you in tomorrow."

I smiled at him and headed for my car, as the sound of approaching ambulance sirens sounded in the distance.

CHAPTER 9

A Step Off the Rung Ladder

Hey um. Hi. Hey. It's uh… me, again. Kevin.

So, it's been a couple weeks but…

Shepard has been…

Well.

Very busy and never had time to…

Fucking hell I can't think straight.

I'm sorry. I haven't been feeling good for a long time. It's going to take an hour just to speak aloud how I feel.

Okay I think I'm ready.

So, two days after our original base got leveled, I got the team settled in at the Overthinker's bunker. We immediately got to work getting prepared for the fight against Harbiter, since he was the next target anyways, just now it was more personal now that he destroyed the old home base and indirectly killed our only explosives master.

I was by myself, in the new office, messing around with computer wires and shit at my new desk. The KOTH was nice enough to provide me a new top of the line computer setup, with 6 cores, two cooling fans, 15 terabytes of storage, 2 terabytes of RAM, several high end video cards, TWO motherboards, and several monitors.

Let me tell you, I get absolutely no slowdown with this beautiful machine.

Hell, I even upgraded the speech to text app so it's more responsive and I'm not taking an hour to write a chapter.

Getting off track again, my bad.

So, while I'm messing about with wires and shit, Shepard comes in all casual like, and I spot his shoes from under the desk. I call out to him, saying, "Shep-my-man, what's up buddy chum pal? You need anything? I got some scotch in the mini fridge if you're interested. If not, there's always the various sodas I get from the quick mart on the edge of town."

Shepard walks over and crouches down to look at me seriously. "Kevin, I have a couple of questions, if it's not too much."

I continue to mess with the wires, prompting him, "Ask away buddy."

He sits down cross legged and pulls out his usual notepad and pen, then asks me the most unexpected and straightforward question I've ever been asked by him; "Kevin, what is your sexual preference? You never told me what side you lean towards."

I stop what I'm doing and give him a weird look. I then tell him matter-of-factly, "I am as straight as it gets, Shepard. There's not a homosexual urge in my body."

Shepard scribbles something down.

"That's interesting to learn, considering how all your employees and even your best friend is male."

I narrow my eyes at him, just a tad bit annoyed. I then start telling him straight up, "Shepard, do you even KNOW what kind of work we are doing? You do realize we are by all legal means, criminals trying to take over a city full of Superhumans?"

He look at me as if he'd just realized that, and kind of looked at the ground awkwardly. I continued telling him off.

"Shepard, basically everyone I've hired, with the exception of Zealot, is a man who is desperate. Either they needed a fucking job and were willing to put their neck out for a decent fucking paycheck, or they were a fucking federal criminal without anything to lose. All these men came to me because they needed a job, or a new lease on life. And to think of it in another way, can you think of one woman, any single self respecting woman, who would willingly put their life on the line for an egotistical jackass like me, doing illegal work such as murder, aggravated theft, destruction of government property, or fuck, illegal arms trade?"

He pursed his lips, staring at his notepad. He then quickly scribbled something else down, and said, "Fair enough Kevin. So… why aren't you with a girl? I would imagine there's lots of girls who'd think a Supervillain with mechanical limbs and an Alpha male superiority complex was extremely hot and worth dating."

I rolled my eyes, and said to him, "I'm just not looking for a relationship right now. Not to mention I don't want a freaking…" I cough harshly, "THOT for a girlfriend. I want a girl I can look in the eye and have her stare back without fear of me. I want a girl who doesn't need me to be there to help her. I want… someone as confident as me, without the ego."

Shepard nodded, scribbling one last thing down, then he closed the notepad and looked at me resolutely.

I looked back, waiting for his next question.

He asked me, staring me down, "What bomb is Seriousman making, Kevin?"

I shook my head rapidly, as if trying to even out my hair, and I looked at him closer. I squinted.

"Shepard. Are you sure you want to know?"

"Kevin, I HAVE to know. You and Blastocyst talk about this bomb as if it spells the end of the world. What are we dealing with?"

I sighed and rubbed my forehead with my right hand.

"Alright, I guess I owe you that much… well Shep, Soups is making a Sub-nuclear quantum destabilization explosive, or just a Sub-Nuclear Bomb for short. You see, Blastocyst developed it as a way to provide a nuclear-level detonation without the radioactive fallout. The bomb is powerful enough to atomize all of Megatropolis with the one detonation. Seriousman has become far too serious about getting rid of Villains. My only concern is, what about civilians in the blast radius? How is he going to get all the people out of the city without tipping off the Villains that something is up?"

Shepard bit his lip, then started chewing on the end of his pen the longer I went on. When I reached the part about civilians and evacuations, he summarized what was on his mind, "So, if we are within city limits when the bomb goes off, we all die?"

I hesitated.

But, I took a breath, and gave him complete honesty, "YOU all will die, Shep. The only ones who would actually survive an atomizing blast like that is Seriousman and… well, me."

His eyebrow went up as he heard that. He put down his pen and said sarcastically, almost as if he wasn't surprised, "Wait, YOU can survive that kind of blast? How?"

I shrugged, "My scientists tell me it's the Faridian adaptation. My body is so tightly woven at the fundamental level, that nothing short of the end of the universe could vaporize me. Now don't take it as immunity to disintegration meaning complete invulnerability. My adaptation works on a case by case basis. I'm told all Faridian based entities automatically have this trait of atomization immunity. I still have to gain all the other forms of immunity, such as ballistic, diseases, toxins, explosives, and damage to specific parts of the body, like eye damage and hearing loss. I also need to be exposed to more and more Faridian until I can walk around with mostly pure Faridian parts on my arm. When I am at that stage, basically nothing can kill me."

Shepard seemed to be satisfied with that huge exposition dump. He looked at me once more, and asked his last question he probably got just then, "How did your scientists MAKE Faridian in the first place?"

I rolled my eyes and said, "They all got fuckin drunk, and they came back to the lab one night, and they started throwing shit together and when they woke up they had a block of pure Faridian the size of a small bike in a crate. Nobody recorded how they did it, and they were too drunk to remember anything. They may be geniuses, but they do idiotic shit from time to time."

Shep scribbled that down, and said his thanks, exiting my office. I sighed and got back to hooking stuff up. Shepard suddenly came back in, carrying a CD player, and he quickly placed the device on my desk, saying quickly, "Oh, almost forgot to give this to you! I got together a bunch of songs I liked and burned them onto a CD, and I had this old CD player I didn't need, so I wanted you to have them. You wanted to know more about my tastes, and this is the most I can provide at the moment... so be sure to listen when you can!"

He quickly exited again, and I was left with struggling to untangle the mess of wires that was my computer setup.

* * * * *

I walked out of my office what felt like a couple hours later, stretching and popping my bones back into place. I yawned, having accidentally fallen asleep. A quick trip down the stairs into the main bunker hangar, and a jog to my scientists across the way who were setting up some weird machinery used to create some of Overthinker's old robots.

I noticed that there weren't all that many guys around, despite it only being a couple hours after my chat with Shep.

I clapped my hands, getting Doc and Browning's attention, and said, "Hey guys! Did I miss anything?"

They just sort of... looked at me. Doc said, "Kevin, you've missed several days of preparation. Did you knock yourself out?"

The world seemed to go quiet.
What?
I checked my arm.
The time, date... it said it hadn't been a couple hours. It had been a couple of DAYS. How the fuck? Did I literally fall asleep for that long? I turned to them, the look of confusion evident on my face. The guys looked at each other, communicating similar thoughts. Browning then told me, "Kevin, your FOCUS might be able to go both ways if you aren't careful. This is probably just one example of that risk. If you've got to sleep, be sure to set an alarm, or have someone you won't automatically kill for waking you up, get you awake, okay? Now you need to go to this address..."

He pulled out a piece of paper and handed it to me, and I looked it over really quick, "And you need to get there as soon as possible. They probably already started the fight against Harbiter and his forces."

I put the paper in the nearby trash can, and I asked the guys, "How the fuck am I gonna get there quickly? I can only go so fast, and I haven't practiced my FOCUS enough to maintain it for very long."

That's when Doc and Browning, in unison, pointed to the machine, with Doc stating, "Hop in, we're going to upgrade your arm and legs."

I raised an eyebrow, but I complied with them, stepping into the midst of the contraption. Doc signaled me to turn around the other direction. I spun about face, and the sound of whirring parts and accessories sounded around me as the complex contraption whirred to life.

My left arm and leg were encased by it, and the machine got to work on upgrading my mechanics.

Doc explained to me what was going on, "Browning and I developed these upgrades in lieu of the fight against Harbiter. Since he is extremely fast, you'll need to be able to keep up with him at the least, or exceed his speed if it comes down to it. So, we came up with an overclocker system for your legs, to amp up your movement speeds to ridiculous levels. In combination with your FOCUS power, you'll be able to possibly reach the light speed barrier, depending on how much you FOCUS, and how fast you run."

Browning took over for the next part, "We are also installing a new plasma cannon and air pressure system in your arm. While yes, the cannon is powerful, it can only be used a couple of times before overheating the gun. As for the air pressure system, you know how air-powered hammers work, yes?"

I thought about it for a moment, and asked, "I guess they use compressed air to output a massive force with the hammer?"

Browning gave a small 'so-so' wave with his hand, and then explained, "Well, you have the right idea. Basically we're going to allow you to amp up your punching power significantly. Doc and I came up with this super strong metal, it's absurd we threw this together, we call it Fallidium. It's extremely resistant to shear force and pressure, to the point where we were able to take a small can that could hold 10 fluid ounces and put over 800,000 TONS PER SQUARE INCH into the can."

My eyes widened. Holy shit, I wasn't an absolute genius like these two, but I knew that once you got past pounds per square inch, you were dabbling in potential mass collateral detonation.

"While the can superheated and caused nuclear fusion inside it, we knew we had to let you have one of your own. Just give the switch on the side a flick, and the vacuum will start inhaling surrounding air. You will need to be careful nobody is around, or no paper is nearby, because the vacuum is going to take in a lot of air really fast, anyone too close will be pulled in and probably get hurt, and loose light stuff will jam the vacuum and activate the emergency shutoff. But once the vacuum finishes, and you'll know it's finished, you can just swing your arm at something and the compressed air will be released out your arm all at once. Anything in front of you, well…"

Browning gave a lighthearted chuckle, "Well, let's say for simplicity's sake that the pressure we set the vacuum to intake was able to break reinforced concrete and turn a cow carcass into giblets."

So that explained why the scientists invited us out for a company barbecue.

I felt really lucky to have hired these two when I did. They've been an investment that repays itself tenfold, in weapons and cool science shit.

I looked at my left arm as the machine finished up with it, and I waved it about a little. It felt significantly heavier than before, and I noticed a small slot on the bottom of my wrist, with a small trigger switch on the bottom. I pressed down on it, and what appeared to be half of a shotgun cartridge slid out of the slot.

I looked at Browning quizzically, who looked at Doc with the same look as me.

I turned to Doc, who cleared his throat, stating, "I know how much you love your 8 gauge, so I took the liberty of adding a mini sized version of the Automated Bullet Generation Module in your wrist, wired specially for the ammo your shotgun uses. You'll be able to reload your shotgun just by swiping your wrist over the bottom loading slot of your shotgun."

I grinned so wide, I had to forcefully stop myself from smiling, I was so full of excitement. My scientists knew no limit to their ingenuity. The parts of the machine holding my legs finished their work overclocking my legs, and let me go, allowing me to step off the platform.

Like my arm, my legs were noticeably heavier, but the overclocker components made my leg movements much smoother, more akin to actual legs than just pillars of titanium alloy.

I jogged over to the soldier's station, where I kept my stuff with the rest of the guys while I waited on installing a shelf into my new office.

I opened the locker, noticed my leftover pastrami and cheese sandwich was suspiciously absent, and I grabbed my 8 gauge out of the locker, slinging it on my back.

I gave a quick wave to Doc and Browning, and I hurried out of the bunker.

Standing outside in the hot sandy sun, I looked down the long stretch of highway that separated me from Megatropolis.

I shifted my weight from foot to foot, and then crouched down, activating my legs.

They rose to life with a whirr. I leaned down and placed my right hand on the asphalt, bracing myself against my legs.

I inhaled.

I exhaled.

I charged my legs.

My whole body was tense.

Then, I FOCUSED.

I rocketed toward the city at blazing speed.

I pumped my legs, running faster than I ever have before. My feet slammed the ground repeatedly, as if they were trying to break through the Earth itself.

I was leaned forward, the wind flowing through my hair, and my teeth, since I had the biggest grin I'd had since probably a few minutes ago. Miles went by in minutes, and I was about to reach the city proper.

I charged my legs again.

But this time I jumped.

With the sound of an airburst and broken pavement, I launched off the ground and into the air, hollering and laughing all the way up and over four buildings on the edge of the city.

I landed flat footed on a building roof, but I immediately launched off of that one, albeit with less force.

And so I flew across the rooftops of the city, bouncing from building to building, making my way toward my guys and the Harbiter's place.

Each jump was an adrenaline rush.

Each landing was a new breath.

And I felt fucking invincible.

Ahhh…. How I wish I felt like that forever.

Arriving at Harbiter's place with a grand entrance, I landed in the courtyard of the city's museum, the museum being the excuse Harbiter called a home base.

I saw while falling that most of the security detail was already dead, goons hired by Harbiter to keep away potential criminals and vandals.

Well instead of normal criminals or vandals, they got two contingents of expertly trained soldiers, a bibliographer with a gun, and now that I've arrived, the city's most dangerous human being.

If I could even be called that at this point, since I lacked a soul and all.

Anyways, the security guards in the front were all dead. Blood was everywhere. A lone janitor who could give less of a shit about the carnage was on the front steps, mopping up a puddle of blood.

I quickly jogged over to him, avoiding blood puddles to keep from annoying him with tracking it everywhere, and I asked him respectfully,

"Hey, do you know where a troop of about fourteen soldiers went from here?"

The old man squinted at me, and continued his mopping, saying dismissively, "Yeah, they went inside, I think they split up indoors. One group went downstairs, which is never a good idea, and the other group is probably scoping out the upstairs."

I smiled, said thanks, and ran inside, stepping over another dead security guy.

Upon entering, I was greeted with a shitload of devastation.

Dead guys were everywhere.

Statues, paintings, glass, was scattered and basically obliterated by stray bullets. I saw a door in the far right corner of the room, leading downstairs given the sign that said, "Basement Level".

There was a grand staircase leading upstairs, more dead folks in the middle of the room, and Squad 1, with good old Steve as head commander. I smiled thankfully and ran over to the group.

Steve waved at me and jogged down to meet me, but he wasn't watching where he was going and tripped over a dead security guy when he was within five feet of me, so I had to catch him and get him back on his feet.

"Whoa there buddy. Almost kneecapped yourself there."

Steve smiled thankfully, and said, "Honestly boss, I never thought you'd wake up. We couldn't just turn back on the plan if you couldn't make it, besides, Zealot made these plans so we could do them without your help."

I rolled my eyes and let him go. "Yes, I know my second in command well enough to know he'd plan for the contingency that I wouldn't show up, Steve. I may act oblivious, but I'm ahead of you on most things."

I looked at the basement door, that was hanging open on one hinge. Steve followed my gaze, and thus my train of thought, informing me the following: "The second squad went down there fifteen minutes ago, and we lost radio contact with them ten minutes ago. In Zealot's plan he detailed that if that were to happen, we weren't supposed to follow, since the likelihood of Harbiter being down there was extremely high.

And as we all know, he refuses to leave his basement on a Friday, due to his OCD."

I frowned and asked, "So, why did Squad 2 get sent down there if we know they have no possible chance of killing him?"

He waggled a finger at me, "Remember Kevin, you're the only one who could possibly move fast enough to catch and kill Harbiter. But while Harbiter is the top priority in this mission, the secondary thing we have to do is disarm or retrieve any weapons of the former Maddest Bomber. That's why Squad 2 was sent down there."

I looked back to Steve. I looked at the stairs.

I looked at Steve.

Then the stairs.

I started jogging for the stairwell without another word.

What remained in my head as I descended into the pristine grey stairway, were the words Steve shouted to me on my way down.

"Think fast and move faster, Kevin! It's the only way to beat him!"

At the bottom of the stairway, I had no idea what to expect. Blood was on the list, but it wasn't the first thing I thought It'd be stepping in.

Splat, splat, my metal feet squished in red human goo. What was on the floor was a pile of meat, armor, and a gun.

I had no idea which of my men was unlucky enough to get this fate, but he seemed to have been effectively vibrated until he got turned to pulp.

Oh the pain he must have suffered.

Don't ask me how I knew that, just roll with it.

I stepped over the puddle and drew my shotgun, raising it up enough so I could make a snapshot if needed.

I proceeded through the basement levels, following the trail of blood on the floor. First turn I came to, I saw another corpse.

This soldier had a hole in his chest, where his rib cage would be.

Find him, slaughter the bastard "hero".

I shook my head, rattling the thoughts of murder and pain from my head, and I kept moving.

Next was two of my guys, both of which died shoved together. No seriously, they were painfully linked together by their ribs.

At least I assumed it was painful, given the looks of agony on their faces.

I'm more human than he will ever be.

I took a deep breath, and powered onward.

I was going to fucking destroy Harbiter.

I made a few more turns, descending deeper into the basement. I came across a few more dead men, each death as gruesome as the last.

One had his spine shoved down his throat.

Kill.

One had all his limbs shot off with his own gun.

Maim.

One had his hips become part of his torso.

BUTCHER HIM.

It was all reminiscent of the SAW movies, or Mortal Kombat fatalities.

But through all the brutal deaths I saw, not a single one of the men were Shepard.

I eventually came across a door in the wall, after two minutes of no bodies to be found.

I approached it slowly, and gently, quietly opened the door...

"AHHH! Stay away! Don't make me shoot!"

I laughed in joy as I recognized the panicked tone of my second best friend, and I swung the door wide open. "SHEPARD! FUCK YES, YOU'RE ALIVE!"

Thank whatever God is listening, he's not dead.

I pushed his gun aside and gave him a relieved hug, receiving a reluctant hug right back. "Oh... h-hey Kevin... it's you... I'm glad you're here..."

He sounded sad almost. I let him go and pulled him to his feet, "Up buddy, tell me, you okay? What happened? How did you get this far without dying horribly?"

He shuddered, choked, and almost broke down, holding his face as he was wracked with traumatized sobbing.

Oh no. He must have somehow hid with the dead.

Poor fucker, didn't expect this much horror in his job.

What could I say? I spoke without thinking. He had just witnessed six good men get turned into fucked up murder art, by a psychopathic man who was equal parts OCD, ADHD, zealous, self-obsessed, anti hero and fucked up sadistic murderer.

If you think I'M bad, well, I don't know what to tell you.

I comforted Shepard as best I could, patting him on the back. But after a short while I had to stir him up from his mourning, as we still had a job to do, and there was a crazed man still somewhere in the basement.

"Come on Shep… there's time for crying later, we gotta kill this fucker. He's the only one we know of with Seriousman's weakness in his personal safekeep. We kill him, then we can go after Seriousman and effectively take over the city for good."

I handed him his gun, helped him up once more, and we started on our way toward our certain future, wherever that ended us up.

And as much as I hate to break it to you, that future wasn't a good one.

In the end, all things will die, even Death himself.

I will probably quote you on that.

CHAPTER 10

Nevermore

Shepard and I walked shoulder to shoulder, our guns raised slightly. The air was stagnant, reeking of mildew, blood, and... charcoal. Later on I'd find out he had occasional barbecues in his private sanctum.

Right then I assumed he just burned bodies down there.

We came to the door leading in, and took position on either side of it. I looked at Shep, nodded, and shoved the door open, with him following close behind.

Ahead of us was Harbiter, standing tall with his hands clasped behind his back, and watching a set of security monitors viewing the entirety of the museum.

Harbiter was wearing his Super costume, a yellow and red bodysuit with a round bold "H" on the back and probably the front, with a non copyright infringing lightning bolt crossing over it.

The monitors showed that the cops had just arrived and were encircling the front entrance, with my men still indoors and taken defensive positions around the main atrium of the museum.

We were running out of time.

I trotted forwards a few steps, my shotgun pointed right at the back of Harbiter's head, and I said demandingly, "Alright fucker. Here's how it's going to go. Either you give us what we came for, or I take your teeth out and use them to write my name into your skull and I take what I want anyways."

He didn't say a thing for a few moments.
But he slightly turned, his blonde hair hiding his eyes but not his grin as he said, malevolently, "Is that so?"
A rush of wind passed by my ear, and he was gone.
Fearing the worst, I spun around, only to watch as Harbiter used my pistol to blow a hole through Shepard's head.

.....

Now hopefully you understand why I was so reluctant to start talking earlier.

.....

Thank God this program detects silence and puts the ellipses in the document for me.

.....

Harbiter dropped my gun, seemingly disgusted with how he killed my BEST FRIEND.
"Ugh… not a clean kill. I could have added more flair maybe… in the eye would have been better. Ah well, there's one left. I'll take my time with you…"

Anger.
So, much, anger.
Burning, seething hatred.
Sure, seeing my men dead was bad enough.
But this?
This was too much.
Shepard TRUSTED me. He trusted me to see him through the mission.
But I failed to act.
And he died. He died because I didn't act.
He.

Died.

And now?

Now I was livid.

My eyes rose to meet Harbiter.

You. YOU. I AM GOING TO MAKE YOU BURN.

I took three steps toward him and took a bullet in the eye.

I growled animalistically, the bullet falling to the ground. The eye it hit was still wide open, and focused on Harbiter.

The yellow clad man had picked my gun up again in the blink of an eye, and shot me, but when it had no effect, he was slightly interested.

"Hmm. So you're bulletproof? No matter."

By that time, I was so focused on him, I was actually FOCUSED.

So FOCUSED in fact, when he dashed at me to strike me in the ribs, I caught his arm midway with my left mechanical hand, stopping him dead in his tracks.

Revenge for the victims.

Time went back to normal, and Harbiter looked up at me in shock. "W-what the hell? Nobody is faster than me..."

I squeezed, hard.

The sound of cracking bones filled the air as I shattered his arm in my hand.

Suffer my pain.

His eyes went wide and he gasped in pain, grabbing at my hand and trying to yank my hand off with his super strength.

But it failed him.

In a panic, he struck at my face, stunning me enough for me to let him go.

Harbiter stumbled over himself trying to run from me, and while he did move faster than a normal human, it wasn't his usual faster-than-the-eye-can-track speed.

I turned and followed after him, my eyes full of burning fury and pointed directly at him.

You cannot stop the reaper.

He retreated to a room adjacent to the security room, and he slammed the door shut behind him, locking and barring it to try and slow me down.

Not a few seconds later the doors screamed as their hinges were torn off.

The doors crashed down, and Harbiter scrambled behind a desk, holding his arm. I'm pretty sure he was panicking because his powers weren't working.

I knew the reason why.

I had my Faridian arm on that day.

And before you ask, yes, I had the organic cover on before going in against Harbiter. I took it off right before opening the door to his security room.

Before he killed Shepard.

Grrr...

I was going to fucking kill him.

Glad to see we agree

My feet clanked against the ground as I walked over to his desk. I grabbed one end and threw it aside, revealing the cowering Superhuman. He scooted backwards as fast as he could, his eyes wide in fear. He screamed at me, "Who ARE you?! How did you take away my powers?! Why are you here?!?!"

I didn't say anything. I just towered over him, my eyes narrowed and glaring down at him.

He got up enough courage to stand and face me, still clutching his broken arm with his free hand. He started to go on one of those stupid monologues talking about how they're the better man and blah, blah, blah. I'll give you the TL;DR version.

"YOU are imperfect! You and your kind are a parasite on society, evil people who need to be made an example of! When all Villains have perished, only then will humanity become a truly great and peaceful society! YOU will lose, because WE are justice! WE are the good guys! And if we have to shed YOUR blood to do it, we will fucking slaughter every one of your kind! No Villain has a place in our new world! None of you!!"

I just continued to stare at him.

He grunted uncomfortably, probably wondering why I didn't strike him down right there and prove his point.

I held out my arms, as if offering him a hug.

Gentle like a butterfly.

He recoiled a bit, but realized I didn't hit him.

I gritted my teeth.

I hollered at him, all my anger bursting out right then, "COME AT ME THEN, YOU FUCKING MONSTER! Show me who is truly evil! If you're the good guy, why haven't you WON yet?!"

He hissed and punched me with his free hand right in my face. He shook his hand that he punched with, gasping in pain when he hit my solid titanium plated skull.

I bent back a bit, blinked, and reset position, barely affected.

I growled again, "Come on! Hit me! Fight me!" I then lowered my voice, smiling a grim, sinister smile, "Give me a hug…"

He raised an eyebrow at me, "R-really?"

I cackled maniacally, wrapping my arms around him and lifting him up, squeezing him.

And I squeezed.

All of his breath left his body as I crushed him, slowly, painfully.

Brutal as a rabid wolf.

I thought about all the shit he did today. All the agony he inflicted in the past. Which made me think… how am I any better for making him suffer?

I came to this realization as I heard his ribs crack.

I am not inhuman.

Well, fuck. Might as well end him here. Not like killing him slowly will make him any less dead.

I have mercy.

After all, I got men to save upstairs.

I dropped him to the floor, letting him take one last painful breath of air before twisting his neck a full 360°, his lifeless body falling to the floor.

I am still a professional, with a child's personality.

I took a breath and FOCUSED, slowing time as much as I could without a reference point. I then scoured the room best I could, looking for any hint of the possible hiding place of Seriousman's weakness.

I even dragged the desk off the wall and looked through it, and still found nothing.

Fuck my life.

At least it doesn't get worse.

He probably already had it destroyed. Harbiter didn't have it.

I'll kill Seriousman anyways.

I ran back upstairs as fast as I could, retrieving my fallen men's identification as best I could.

Remember the fallen as I have fallen.

In the meantime, I carried Shepard's limp body on my shoulder, all the way through the basement levels, up the stairs to the main atrium, and to my relief it seemed I stopped time as the firefight broke out between the authorities and my men.

I put Shepard's body down, and cracked the knuckles on my right hand, my anger turned to resolution.

I had a fight to end, and now.

No more need to die.

I started working out where all the bullets were going from each side. All the bullets from the Swat and so on I just removed from the air with my metal arm, removing all their momentum immediately.

After getting rid of all the opposing bullets, I went to each of the cops and took their guns right out from their hands. I even went so far as to steal their sidearms and backups in the SWAT trucks and local police vehicles, I had to be thorough.

An unarmed opponent is a beaten one.

When I removed all the opposing side's guns and moved them to the info kiosk where three of my guys were using it as cover, I then went and stood in the midst of the two groups, my team of seven or so remaining men versus a whole battalion of now unarmed local law enforcement.

I closed my eyes and unfocused.

The sound came back to the world as my men leveled over half the police squadron, who had come to realize that their guns were all gone for some unknown reason.

Steve eventually noticed this as well, and signaled the guys to quit firing.

The last bullet casings fell to the ground, and I stood alone, facing the large group of police and SWAT members.

Some debating sprung up in the midst of the law enforcement, and eventually an adult woman about as tall as me (5' 11"), came out and approached.

A strong leader like me.

She walked right up to me and looked me dead in the eye, and asked, "Who are you, Villain?"

I met her gaze, feeling very, very exhausted all of a sudden. I believe the use of my FOCUS had some hand in that, but I also think the fatigue of losing Shepard that day also took its toll. I replied, my fatigue showing, "My name is Kevin Andréson. And you plus your men are all unarmed and completely helpless. You're really lucky I'm not in the mood for killing any more people today because I would have gladly done so if I hadn't witnessed a total fucking nightmare five minutes ago, thanks to your 'Hero' Harbiter. I got what I came for, I just want to take my men, and my only remaining dead who isn't mutilated beyond recognition, and go home. So if you would be so kind, as to get out of our way, we will leave and not cause any more trouble."

Good, make yourself non-threatening.

She glared at me with the kind of mistrust you would expect. But I guess something in my eyes told her I was being honest. She pulled up her walkie talkie and spoke into it, "Alright boys, the leader says he wishes to leave in peace, and I believe him. We don't have a choice anyway, DAVE, before you say anything. No, I— DAVE, DON'T MAKE ME TELL THE SUPERVILLAIN TO MURDER YOU. No? Nothing? Oh, Dave's dead? How?!"

Fix their problems, make yourself seem helpful.

I coughed and winked at her, and she got the hint, saying into the mic again, "Nevermind then, just let them go. No we aren't going to avenge DAVE, he was literally a parasite to our team. Let it go Tommy. Good boy."

She turned back to me, and said, harshly, "Get out. I better not see your face again."

I turned around, and called to the guys, "ALRIGHT BOYS, let's get the fuck out of here, and NOW."

Leave before it gets worse.

Steve and the remainder of the guys grouped up and ran for the vans, piling into one of them as I quickly ran for Shepard's body, taking a moment and looking through his pockets to see if I could find maybe any information, like his ID or social security number.

I didn't know much about his past. I wanted to learn more about my former best friend's past. While I searched his pockets, I found a small note in his coat pocket. I shoved that in my own pocket, along with his wallet and key ring.

Everything can be useful.

I then picked him up, and ran for the van, just as the guys were starting it up. I quickly got there and lay Shep in the van, when suddenly I felt my waist get grabbed and I was sent flying into the air, with no control over my movement.

Great, it gets worse.

Where did the fucking ground go?!

I writhed and twisted, trying to see what the fuck grabbed me, and I managed to turn around enough to get a knee in my chest, sending me higher into the air. Winded, I coughed harshly, until I felt my ascent slow.

Then I felt another strike against me, this one sending me flying in the direction of the Dunes.

Great day for a tan.

I hate the sun!

I felt the wind screaming past my ears, as I careened toward the light brown sands. Another strike midair sent me flying faster toward the sands. When I eventually hit the ground at extremely high speeds, I felt some of my skin on my back receive an extreme sandburn. I skipped across the sand, eventually sliding to a stop maybe several miles outside the city limits.

My back was in pain for a moment, but my adaptation and regeneration made the pain ebb away, until it was all gone. I dragged myself to my feet, when I felt a blast of sand hit me dead in the face. I grunted and looked up to see the unmistakable figure of a floating man in a black and grey superhero suit, a big non-copyright infringing "S" embroidered on the front of his suit.

It's this fucking pleb again.

Rip his head off.

He glared down at me with the same superiority complex afflicted look that Harbiter gave me before I broke his arm.

I shrugged my shoulders and popped my neck back into place, addressing him frankly, "Sup, Soups? I figured you would have to show up eventually."

He angled his head down to look at me more directly. "Mister Andréson, I'm not surprised you would have showed up to Harbiter's place just to kill him the way you did. Then again, he did obliterate your men like they were nothing and left them as if they were museum displays. My condolences, no man, Villain or not deserves to experience something like that."

He's lying, punch his fucking teeth in.

Patience. His confidence will be his death.

I raised my eyebrow at him, "Huh, that's literally the most sentimental thing I've ever heard you say Soups. Thanks, I guess."

To put this whole situation into context, me and Seriousman have encountered each other before, but those were only ever in public, when he was giving speeches or casually seeing fans and civilians. We kinda had a rivalry going, where I would harass him and he would restrain himself, but this was the most blatantly close to a fight that we've come. And considering how he threw the first blow today, I had a feeling we were going to come to blows in a moment.

Foreshadowing at its finest.

He snorted and rolled his eyes, telling me in an annoyed tone of voice, "Just because I did a soup commercial ONCE doesn't mean you're allowed to call me 'Soups', Andréson! I am Seriousman, the world's greatest Superhero!"

I shrugged, saying in a voice that dripped with sarcasm, "Yeah and I'm the mayor of Megatropolis. Well, I'm not, yet."

More foreshadowing. Keep up the combo.

He narrowed his eyes at me, "You will never take over this city. Not while I still stand, Villain."

I looked at him, feeling very tired all of a sudden. I wasn't in the mood for his shit, honestly…

"Look pal, I got dead to bury. And if we're gonna fight, we might as well—"

Bam! Clash!

Welp, there goes subtlety.

MURDER HIM.

He dashed at me, swinging for my chest, but I dodged left, avoiding his swing and I countered with a left hook, slamming my Faridian fist into his face, stumbling him and making him hover backwards, a look of impression on his face, along with an impression of my fist.

"Hrrn. You're fast, Mister Andréson. I admit, you would have to be in order to beat Harbiter."

Understatement.

I clenched my right hand.

"Not necessarily, Seriousman."

Let's fucking go.

Seriousman rolled his eyes again, and we went at each other. To anyone else looking on at us it would have seemed like a blur of fists and kicks, but in our relative perception it was like time hadn't changed. He was the one mostly swinging at me, while I blocked, dodged and countered his strikes, trying to expose him to my mechanical arm as much as possible.

Drain him, outlast him.

I had no idea if the Faridian exposure would be the same as exposing him to whatever radioactive alien rock that was his weakness, but I had to try and see if it would work.

Eventually he got in a blow strong enough to send me flying onto my back, but I didn't go far at all. I was able to get back to my feet as he stood there, glaring at me in annoyance.

I just want to bite his throat and rip it out.

Dude, chill out.

Fuck you!

He hovered in the air once again, drawing in some sort of energy from the air, gathering light within himself. He boomed out in a voice that was much deeper and louder than his normal voice, "This is where you die, Kevin. I shall unleash the power I have been endowed with by Mother Nature herself. I shall destroy you with the power of our endlessly powerful sun!"

He began glowing and shouting loudly, charging up an attack. He gathered a ball of energy and fire in his hands, and yelled, "Planet Cracker, Hyper-beam!!"

Hmm. My scientists knew more than I could have ever guessed.

Shoulda known he had a laser.

With a flourish of his arms he directed the beam at me and fired it off.

I will give you three guesses as to what I did, and if you got the first two wrong, they don't count.

Got your answer? Sure it's the one you want?

Okay.

I closed my eyes and FOCUSED.

After slowing time to a crawl (or more accurately, accelerating myself too fast for time to handle), I simply walked around and stood behind Seriousman, unfocusing and letting his huge ass laser beam loose.

Not bad, stylish and practical.

With the sound of a thousand roaring jet engines, the beam shot off into the distance, actually even splitting the clouds in the far distance.

I leaned on Soup's shoulder, waiting for him to stop.

After he was finished, he looked at me with wide eyes.

He's scared. We have him

I pretended to polish the nails of my right hand on my shirt, patting his shoulder with my Faridian arm, "Not bad, that was flashy as fuck boy. Nine outta ten, could use more targets than the poor dune beetles in the way."

He grabbed me and we went careening across the wastes, with him punching and striking me in pure anger, while I took the hits and dished them back twice as hard, fighting him like a rabid honey badger.

Bleed, BLEED YOU BASTARD.

He eventually resorted to dragging me through the sand, trying to use the abrasive sand particles to scrape my flesh off. Thanks to my regeneration and adaptation, I was mostly unaffected, but it still hurt like a motherfucker.

Ow ow ow ow ow ow ow

FUCK FUCK FUCKING MOTHERFUCKER FUCK YOU FUCKING BITCH ASS—

He soon picked me out of the sand and threw me at a wall of sand, letting me impact it at ridiculous velocity.

He then crashed into me, and I swore I felt something snap inside me, but I still felt fine even if it felt like I got rug burns.

I think it was the lower second rib.

I pulled myself out of the sand, staring at him with a gaze of knives.

He started panting, breathing heavily from exhaustion. He wiped a bit of blood off his face.

I tilted my head and smiled, feeling almost sadistic as I said, "Huh. I always thought you were 'invincible', Soups."

It's actually working, like I hoped.

He grimaced and stood up straight, looking me dead on, his voice unwavering as he said, "Justice will never die, Kevin. You may have weakened me in some way, but you cannot—" I cut him short by punching him really hard with my left arm.

You will die like the rest, asshole.

He stumbled backwards, blood spurting from his nose. He covered it to try and stem the bleeding, and fell to one knee. I heard him mumble under his breath, "How? I have only one weakness, yet I still feel fatigued and drained of power…"

His only option was to get out of there before I murdered the crap out of him, so he went with it.

Seriousman got to his feet and flew off, albeit with a wobbly trajectory, toward Megatropolis. I stared after him, my thoughts all floating about in my head.

Eventually two absolute thoughts came into my head.

1) **Go home, bury Shep, and hide away until I'm needed.**

2) *Get my own fucking house, with my own bed, and everything.*

I was sick of everything.

I wanted to mourn.

But, errands must be done.

So, I pulled out the first thing in my pocket my hand came into contact with: the piece of paper Shepard had with him. I proceeded to unfold it, then read what it said.

It said, "Remember!!! Tell Kevin how to disarm the SN-bomb——> Cut the power!!!"

My eyebrow raised in mild amusement. Then it fell in sorrow. God, Shep. If only you got to tell me yourself.

I put the paper in my other pocket then took out his wallet, and looked through it.

Debit card given to him for his job with me: useless.

$15 cash: Useful for small purchases and maybe a sandwich at the Frontier Deli.

Speaking of he had a punch card for the deli. He was apparently a regular because all but two of the slots were punched out, and he needed to purchase ten sandwiches and get a full meal on the house when he turned in a fully punched card.

I would probably make use of that. What else did he have…

A receipt for a barber shop?

Someone might remember him there too, but the Frontier Deli was a better bet.

I could go for a pastrami and cheese right now. >~<

Please don't make that face ever again.

Old employee card for a former job at the local newspaper. Well, at least he didn't lie about his first name, because it was the same on here. But his last name? Hoohh. I don't think I even know what region of the world that's from.

If you've never seen an apostrophe over an "e" before, your brain would fry upon seeing his last name.

Hisss! Get it away!

Good Lord, that's a mental overload.

I shook my head and continued.

Couple more receipts… a credit card…

Ah, finally. His friggin ID.

Wait.

Fuck this doesn't help me at all. It literally tells me everything I already know about him (Huh, he comes from Illinois, that's interesting to learn tho). Ah well… I remember his address, so that's my next destination.

I put everything back in my pockets, charge my legs, and rocket toward the city, leaving a plume of sand in my wake.

God bless my scientists, I am never taking these legs off.

CHAPTER 11

So Long and Thanks for the Bird

Shepard's apartment was harder to find than expected. I actually passed by it on accident several times before a nice lady pointed me right to it, resulting in me smacking myself in the face.

I walked into the apartment complex, to find it wasn't exactly high class. Then again, midtown Megatropolis was never really high class to begin with. It was a drag of slums and urban settlements where the town government thought it was a good idea to build sewer pipes leading nowhere, and they never bothered cleaning up or regulating the damn place.

So it was a total shitshow from Banker Avenue to Main Street, and from Malcolm King Boulevard to the god damn industrial district.

I would have some serious work to do come my eventual conquering of the city. With Z still here I might have a chance at doing everything I want to do. Hopefully...

I shook these thoughts from my head, they weren't going to get anything done. I looked at his apartment key's number really quick—256— and headed up the stairs, the floors creaking loudly under my several hundred pound body (Faridian Steel tends to weigh in the ballpark of 380 pounds per cubic foot, with normal steel being heavier while the alloy is lighter with the added Faridian).

I came up to the door I wanted, and unlocked the door, opening it. Suddenly squawking could be heard from across the room, as Shepard's bird started hollering at the intruder. I looked at my left arm, suddenly realizing it was fully exposed and dangerous to bystanders. I used the built in system manager to check and see if there was anything my lab boys added to maybe make the Faridian not be exposed.

My search bore fruit, as I found an option to change my arm to "passive" mode. I changed the setting to "activate" and with whirring sounds my arm shifted its parts around until only solid steel was visible. I grinned happily, flexing the finger rotors, and I went over to little Stu, opening the cage and letting him out.

The bird flew on to my mechanical shoulder, settling down on it. Figuring he was hungry I searched around and found some bird feed, using the small grain to fill his bird feed dish with a spoon.

Stu hopped down next to the dish and pecked away at the grain, tweeting randomly as he ate. I noticed he had a water dispenser in his cage, and it was half full, so I don't need to worry about the poor birdy being dehydrated.

Aww, he was a good birb. Such a cute little birb, I adored him.

I *have* been here before, just under different circumstances. Mostly it was just me dropping by to see Shep and see what he was up to and usually he was on his sofa watching a cooking channel or something. I got to play with his little birb Stu as we had a beer together.

Reminds me of the old "cracking open a cold one with the boys" meme from not a year ago.

Although it's more appropriate for when I cracked a cold one with my soldiers.

In my nostalgic stupor, a female voice came from the doorway behind me, "Oh, hello. What are you doing here? Are you one of Shepard's friends?"

I turned and saw a moderate sized woman with black hair, the kind of black you'd see on leather seats. She was similar enough looking to Shep that I could deduce she was family, and young enough that she was probably his sister, since I knew he never married.

And I silently high fived myself when she continued her introduction with, "It's nice to meet you, I'm Mary, Shepard's sister."

I smiled warmly at her, and said to her, "Hello Mary. I'm Kevin, Shep's… former employer. It's nice to meet you."

She looked worried and covered her mouth, saying quietly, "Oh no, *former?* He didn't get fired, did he? What happened?"

The smile fell off my face as I realized I couldn't lie to her. My own biology would betray me if I tried.

To explain, whenever I try to lie, to anyone, about anything, I start uncontrollably laughing and giggling like an idiot. If you remember earlier when I told Blastocyst that I make it obvious when I lie, that's what happens to make it obvious.

I don't know what it was that made it so I was psychologically programmed to laugh when I told a lie, but it made me the most honest I could ever be. But it also forced me into lots of situations where being able to lie would have been a godsend.

I waved her towards the sofa, telling her politely, "Please, sit down. What I'm about to tell you is extremely serious. I don't want you to fall over and hurt yourself accidentally."

She and I sat beside each other on the couch, and I took a moment to compose myself before telling her the story.

"I don't know if Shep told you, but he was hired to do some really dangerous work for me. I recruited him for a couple of reasons, but that doesn't matter, what matters is he was often placed in very dangerous positions in the line of duty."

I bit my lip before telling her outright, "Shepard died today. He was shot in the head by one of the city's 'Superheroes', people who swore to protect the citizens of Megatropolis and the world."

She was speechless. She looked down at the floor, tears welling up in here eyes as she heard something nobody in their right mind wanted to hear. She covered her face and sobbed quietly to herself, leaving me to stare out the window into the far distance.

I noticed then that Shepard had an uncanny good view of the tower in the center of the city, the tower that was built in Seriousman's honor. It was designed in a similar way to the Space Needle in Seattle, with a saucer on top, but the difference between them was 1) This tower had multiple floors in between ground and the top floor, and 2) the top floor was Seriousman's home, inaccessible except for a maintenance stairwell that was locked off from the public.

Oh yeah, and this tower was several times taller than the Space Needle.

After a few minutes of awkward silence, Mary turned to me and tapped on my shoulder, "Hey, I… I need to know… did my brother at least do well at his job? It would make me feel a little better to know if he… if he did…"

I turned back to her, nodding solemnly, "Yes, he did a great job, Hell, an *amazing* job as my bibliographer. Despite the stress and risks he took working with us, he kept his cool throughout. He was a professional, and I respect him all the more for it."

She smiled thankfully at me, "Th-thank you… I feel much better knowing he died doing something he enjoyed. You seem to be very fond of him, and it makes me glad he made a new friend."

She then did something I never anticipated. She fuckin hugged me. Like, seriously. Just leaned over and hugged me as if I'd known her all my life.

I frowned a bit, since I wasn't a fan of physical contact of any form that I didn't initiate. If anything I would be pushing this woman away from me, but she was mourning her family, so I made an exception.

I gently patted her on the back with my right hand, trying to be sentimental. I was tired. I was ready to go home.

She soon enough let me go, and snuffled a bit, "Thank you for being honest, sir. I was supposed to meet my brother for lunch today with our mom, but it seems I'll be going alone today. Looks like I'll have to break the news to poor ma…"

I nodded, then remembered that I had something. The $15 cash.

I pulled it out of my pocket and handed it to her, saying to her, "Hey, I found this on Shepard's person when I was looking for anything that could be given to a close relative. I think he was planning to use this for your lunch."

She covered her mouth again, eyes wide with grief, but a bit of joy as well. "Oh Sheppy… even in death you find a way to pay for my lunch…"

She took the cash from me slowly, holding it close to her chest.

She got up and walked away, but before exiting the apartment, she whistled at Stu, who flew over and perched himself on her shoulder. She gave me one last sad smile, and left for good.

I sat there for another good hour or so, staring at Shepard's small but functional TV. I felt a twinge of remorse for Mary and her mom. Given how I didn't have parents, I wondered what it would be like to talk to a grieving mother.

Hmm? What was that? How did my parents die?

Well, good question, I killed both their sorry asses.

That's a good story for later.

I eventually left that old apartment, locking the door behind me. I went downstairs and left Shep's key on the rack downstairs.

I went home.

CHAPTER 12

How Far I've Come

I don't know how long I laid there, staring at the wall, drifting in and out of sleep.

Days had passed, and time, it felt, was meaningless.

I didn't want to go anywhere.

I didn't want to do anything.

I was so… empty. It was like when I was first crippled, my arm and legs gone in a day.

But this time it hurt me emotionally.

Losing Shepard had a dark and depressing effect on me. What I thought was weird, was that nobody came to check in on me that whole time.

Maybe they just didn't want me to wake up angry or something.

Zealot's family liked me as much as they could like a Supervillain. Zealot's sister only tolerated me because of Zealot's respect for me. And her daughter, while the most precious child on the planet, didn't like me because I was mean to everyone, and I once accidentally set one of her toys on fire, but that's something she got over when I got her ice cream.

I lay there in bed for so long my bones and muscles started to ache, what was left of them anyways.

Then Zealot came in to get me.

He opened the door slowly, the light from outside the room shining into my dark room, casting a line over my back.

I reflexively curled up a bit, but tried not to move so much.

Z came in, softly calling to me, "Kevin? Kevin, you alright?"

I didn't answer.

He walked over to me, and gently shook my shoulder. "Kevin, get up. This is important."

Whatever it was, it didn't need me. I stayed still, and slowly drifted back into my dark sleep.

Z took his hand off me and stepped back a few feet.

"ON YOUR FEET SOLDIER, WE HAVE WORK TO DO!"

I was shocked out of my stupor, and out of reflex I complied with his order and got to my feet, standing straight up and facing him.

He started pacing in front of me, brooding and growling his annoyance at me as he did so, "Now I don't know what the fuck has gotten into you, but this 'poor me, I'm gonna be sad and hide away' attitude is UNACCEPTABLE. You may have lost an important friend, Kevin, but that should NOT stop you from pushing onward and finishing your mission the same as you would if Shepard was still alive! We are on a TIME CLOCK dammit! Whatever it is that is making you like this, GET OVER IT, and come downstairs! You have FIVE MINUTES KEVIN, I better see you then!"

He stormed out of my room, leaving me with my thoughts and the door wide open.

I considered what Zealot was telling me right then. And after talking with myself a bit, I eventually concluded that he was right. I can't waste anymore time mourning. I've got a fight to win. Shepard believed I could pull through and take the city, I can't let him down by failing. I have got to win.

I still had Zealot anyways, one friend was better than none.

With newfound willpower, I ran downstairs and found Zealot standing in the living room, alone, with the TV paused on a news recording. When he heard my footsteps right behind him, he resumed the DVR.

It was a report from earlier this morning. Seemed like a couple hours ago.

"And we are live with Sharon Dullweg on the scene at the I-47 highway headed east, and she will explain more of the situation, to you, Sharon"

The camera swapped to a lady in a helicopter, hovering over the highway that was jam packed with cars, all exiting the city, albeit impressively at a snail's pace.

The reporter started speaking, "Yes, Darrel, the sudden warning broadcast from Seriousman's tower took all of Megatropolis by surprise, with Seriousman himself ordering a mass evacuation of the city, due to a nuclear-level bomb threat in the center of town. Seriousman says he is going to try and defuse the situation as best he can, and we can only hope, he will be able to stop the bomber before it is too late."

Holy Almighty.

I couldn't believe that Seriousman came up with such an ingenious plan like this. First, he removed civilians from the possible collateral damage by ordering an evacuation. Second, he'd make it sound like some crazy terrorists were trying to blow up the city or something. By doing that, and emphasizing he was going to be "defusing" the situation, he'd make the Villains all think, "Oh, Seriousman is going to stop the bomber no problem, he's the Superhero, he always wins."

When in fact he's the one actually setting the bomb off. When enough time passed so the civilians all got far enough away, he'd set off the bomb, and make it look like he was unable to disarm it in time. He'd kill every single Villain in the blast radius who was too used to a world where the Hero always won, and make it look like someone else's fault at the same time.

Jesus Christmas this was more diabolical than any Devil I'd ever met.

Zealot paused the news cast and turned to me, the most serious I've ever seen him.

He said bluntly, "That was several hours ago. By now most of downtown has been evacuated. It will take us 30 minutes to get to the center tower, with the whole of Squad One. We need to get in there and stop him before it's too late."

I nodded at him, and gave him a thumbs up, "Let's go then, what are we waiting for?"

I ran to the door and threw it open to find my soldiers all lined up in a row, all the remaining 6 of them.

Wait, 6? Steve was missing.

I looked at them questioningly, "Wait, where's Steve? I would imagine he'd be here at a time like this."

One of my guys piped up, "Steve said he had some family he had to get out of the city as soon as possible sir!"

I looked back at Z who had just finished locking up the house. He raised his eyebrows at me. We had the same thought at the same time.

Steve doesn't HAVE a family.

I turned back to the guys, and gave a small speech, "Okay guys. Here's how it's going to go. No man wants to die willingly if they think they're going to lose. You all are good men, and have done me a great service all these years, a couple of you I think even came from my old days as a gang leader."

Two of the guys smiled to themselves, and I nodded to them both. I continued, "But this is something I'm not going to require any of you to follow me on. This is my fight, and were you all to come with me, it would be more for my morale than anything. I don't want you to die for me like sheep. You are humans. You deserve to make that choice for yourselves. So who's coming with me?"

They all drew their guns and stood at ease, as one of them said aloud, "We are all coming with you, sir! We got this far, we're fighting at your side till the end!"

All my men shouted at the same time, "TO THE END!"

I grinned like a madman. "Who's driving?"

Zealot tossed the keys to the van up in the air, walking towards it, and caught them as they fell, "I am. You all, get in the back."

I looked at the back of his head in curiosity, wondering why he was coming, but then shrugged. He would know how to disarm the bomb, he's my second in command for a reason.

All the guys filed into the back, and I hopped in with them, closing the doors as Zealot started the van and revved the engine.

* * * * *

We traveled in silence mostly. Zealot wasted no time in putting us all into an 80 mile per hour race towards the center of town.

I stood as per usual, in the usually cramped van that was now more spacious due to the sudden loss in soldiers.

I stared at the back of the van, the engine growling loudly like a bear as it raced down the main drag.

I looked at each of the guys in turn, remembering their names and specialties to pass the time.

Vladimir, general combat specialist. Expert with assault weapons and rigging scrap into attachments for guns. About as Russian as you get, drinking vodka and wearing heavy clothes, but never talked.

Craig, our demolitionist and trap master. I picked him up in my earlier years for the old gang. A street rat turned into a mayhem causing badass.

Dvon, our handgun specialist and weapon tutor. The second guy who was originally from the first gang, his draw was known as one of the fastest on the street. I was glad I had him on my side.

Joseph, the heavy weapons guy. While he preferred to be in full juggernaut body armor and carry a minigun, it was too heavy, loud, and impractical for normal use, so we had him use a modified M-230 LMG instead, with plated body armor to protect against small and medium munitions.

Trevor, our sniper. He was originally a hitman, until Zealot recruited him for a long term job, and even though his contract expired a year ago, he stuck around. Reliable, Irish, speaks when he needs to, and makes a killer sandwich.

And finally, Eric.

He was… how do you say it… eccentric? Yeah that's the word. I ran into him on the side of the road one day holding a sign that said, "Will slay infidels for Jerusalem", with a bastard sword propped up beside him.

This fucking guy runs into fights with his sword, whom he calls Hagatha, and starts slaughtering people while screaming "DEUS VULT" over and over. Naturally we had him be our melee expert, with the promise that we'd eventually help him "reclaim the holy land". He was a laugh and a half, but he killed people without hesitation, at least as long as we called them infidels.

Somehow, as a group of misfits and crazy maniacs, we got to this point, and yet we all were quiet.

I really wanted to break the silence.

So I did. With music.

I took a deep breath, and started singing softly.

"I woke up at the start of the end of the world,

But it's feeling just like every other morning before.

Now I'm wondering what my life is gonna mean when it's gone.

The cars are moving bout a half a mile an hour and I,

Start staring at the passenger's who're waving goodbye,

Can you tell what was ever really special about me all this time?

Well I, believe, the world, is burning to the ground, oh well, I guess, we're gonna find out.

Let's see how far we've come.

Let's see how far we've come."

I drifted off, staring at the floor. Suddenly, Vladimir started giving a beat. The exact beat of that song I was singing.

Joseph continued where I left off.

"I believe it all, is coming to an end, oh well, I guess, we're gonna pretend!

Let's see how far we've come.

Let's see how far we've come."

Trevor starts giving the guitar sounds as I continue the next verse, our team becoming a sort of band in the back of the van.

"I think it turned ten o'clock, but I don't really know,

Then I can't remember caring for an hour or so,

I started crying and I couldn't stop myself,

I started running but there's nowhere to run to!"

Eric picked up the next part, "I sat down on the street, took a look at myself, said 'where you going man you know the world is headed for Hell!

Say your goodbyes if you've got someone you can say goodbye to!"

All who weren't making instruments started singing at once:

"I, believe, the world, is burning to the ground, oh well, I guess, we're gonna find out!

Let's see how far we've come. (Right now)

Let's see how far we've come.

I, believe, it all, is coming to an end, oh well, I guess, we're gonna pretend!

Let's see how far we've come. (Aww yeah!)

Let's see how far we've come."

Everyone got quieter as we got to the third part, a gentle tapping on Eric's sword accompanying our quietness.

I returned to singing eventually, "Well it's gone, gone, baby it's all gone, there's no one on the corner and there's no one at home.

It was cool, cool, it was just all cool, now it's over for me, and it's over for you.

(Two more join in) Well it's gone, gone, baby it's all gone, there's no one on the corner and there's no one at home.

It was cool, cool, it was just all cool, now it's over for me, and it's over for you…"

A pause in the music, then we suddenly start at full speed on the chorus:

"I, believe, the world, is burning to the ground, oh well, I guess, we're gonna find out!

Let's see how far we've come. (Ahhh yea!)

Let's see how far we've come.

I, believe, it all, is coming to an end, oh well, I guess, we're gonna pretend!

Let's see how far we've come. (Aww yeah!)

Let's see how far we've come.

Let's see how far we've come.

Let's see how far we've come.

Let's see how far we've come.

Let's see how far we've come.

Let's see how far we've come!

Let's see how far we've come!

Let's see how far we've come…"

And we ended as we turned onto the last stretch of road.

A moment later, Zealot parked us on the curbside, killed the engine then went around, opening the doors and letting everyone out the back. I hopped down onto the concrete, walking towards the massive fuckin tower.

We all jogged toward it, and I kicked open the reception door.

I probably saved us a minute by doing that as the door was barred from the inside, and I basically bypassed it altogether.

Inside were a handful of looters snatching whatever valuables that weren't tied down.

Three of them, all armed with guns, pointed them at us and opened fire.

I rolled my eyes and FOCUSED, running at the guys who were armed and dangerous. The yells of shock slowed to a halt as time started falling behind me. I did the usual, grabbing bullets, guns, and people, disposing of all of them.

The people I gathered together and tied up in the middle, using the rope they were using to drag and carry heavy objects, and imparted enough force on their heads to knock them clean out.

When all was done, I unfocused, letting my guys fire at nothing before realizing that all the looters were tied together right in front of them.

I waved them all over, and told them all, "Alright, you guys all keep an eye on these bastards for a moment, okay? Me and Zealot need to get up to the top floor as quick as possible to stop Seriousman's bomb. Make sure nobody enters or leaves this building, got it?"

My men all saluted, and spread out, four of them watching the windows while leaving two to stand over the looters.

Zealot and I ran for the elevator, and to no one's surprise, it was shut and inactive. I shrugged at Z after attempting to wrench the doors open, only to find the elevator wasn't even on the bottom floor.

Zealot huffed a disappointed sigh, ran over to an unlabeled door, and pointed at it, telling me, "Alright, kick this door."

I went over, took a good look at it, reeled back and kicked the door right at the handle.

With a loud groan and pop, the door flew open.

Me and Z walked into a massive fucking maintenance stairwell. I looked up at the endless sets of stairs, that went up and up and up.

I grunted and said to Z, "Well, I can get up there easily, but what about you?"

Zealot assessed the situation, a flat yet focused look on his face. After a moment he said, "Think you can carry me?"

I looked at him weird, but when I realized what he was saying, a grin stretched across my face. "You afraid of falling, or heights buddy?"

He shook his head no, still staring up at the tall ass stairwell.

I looked up, and FOCUSED, just enough so I'd have ample time to react, but not enough that if I launched into the air it would hurt Z.

I swept him off his feet, holding him in a regular carry, and launched off the ground, carrying him up several floors before I landed on one side of the stairs, only to launch off that, ascending higher and higher with each jump.

The slow motion helped me a lot with covering a lot of height in a small amount of time.

Eventually we had reached the top floor, and only a minute or so had passed. I set him down on his feet, and unfocused, allowing him to get his bearings. He looked back down, nodding, impressed. "Not bad Kevin. Didn't even get whiplash. You're gonna go far in transportation."

I laughed and opened the next door, waving him through, "Don't think I'm gonna be giving people regular Ubers around town now, these legs were meant for walking."

He walked through, and I walked into the dimly lit hallway, closing the door behind me.

Upon turning back, I saw the outline of a dark figure.

I squinted. Wait. That was one of our uniforms.

I said aloud, feeling extremely confused, "Wait, Steve? Is that you?"

It WAS Steve.

But I didn't expect what Zealot said next.

"Hello, Commando Steve. It's been too long, hasn't it?"

My jaw nearly dropped.

Holy fuck. It made sense. Steve knew we wouldn't believe he would be dumb enough to walk into my base and use his real name to sign up for my conquest of Megatropolis. So he did, and he was so good at leading I made him Squad 1's leader.

He was a mole all along.

I felt like a huge fucking idiot.

Probably warned Harbiter and Seriousman about what we were doing this whole time.

I had to give him and Seriousman credit. They had us outplayed for a long time.

Steve crossed his arms, and glared at Zealot. "It's been more than just 'too long' Zealot. I have waited for years to have my vengeance for the entirety of my platoon in Vietnam. You killed them all. But you didn't kill me." He struck a dramatic combat pose, trying to be intimidating.

Zealot stood, his hands behind his back, about as professional now as he always is, "I didn't touch your fellow soldiers Commando. Your men walked into every trap the Vietcong laid out for them, it was their fault only that they all died."

Steve hissed angrily, "Don't feed me lies, General! We should have won that war, but were it not for you, most of my men would be alive today! Now you'll pay for every ounce of blood you've spilled, by my hand!"

He ran at Zealot, swinging at his face.

Zealot simply sidestepped him and smacked him open palmed in the face.

Steve backed up, then roundhouse kicked at Zealot, only to have his leg grabbed and his whole balance thrown off, sending him to the floor.

Steve hopped to his feet, and started cautiously swinging at my second in command.

Honestly, it felt like Zealot was barely trying. He dodged Steve's swings mostly, and when Steve tried to go for a harder swing, Zealot would counter with a literal slap.

Steve got more and more pissed off the more the fight stalled. When he hit his boiling point, he tried jumping off the wall for a full force double footed kick right at Zealot.

Zealot caught Steve, then batista bombed the poor guy, making me laugh like an idiot how trashed Steve got. Zealot walked over Steve's stunned body, and I jogged after him, laughing and telling Z how awesome that was.

Steve got to his feet, and said screw it to messing around. He pulled out a gun and fired it at Zealot's back.

The bullet hit flesh.

I dropped the bullet on the ground, my right hand having only a slight red mark on it where the bullet hit.

I glared at Steve, the look in my eyes obvious. 'Get the fuck out of here.'

Steve dropped his gun, and walked out the other door, clutching his ribs like a wounded dog.

I turned back around and headed for the other door.

Zealot followed a bit behind, and asked me, "Why did you catch that bullet?"

I said bluntly, "I'm not about to fail again."

He then stated, "You know I wear thick Kevlar, correct? That bullet wouldn't have done anything to me."

I stated back, "I know. I was making a point."

I swung open the next door, to find a beautifully terrifying sight in front of me. First off, Seriousman had great taste in decorations. It was all a good white marble theme, I liked it a lot.

Second, the view was stellar. The city looked amazing from up here.

Third, the bomb was not three meters away, a big block of steel held aloft by a table.

Seriousman stood next to it, staring at the timer.

I could see it from this angle, we had five minutes left.

I stepped forward a few steps, and said to him, "Alright asshole. This is where it ends. If you surrender quietly, I won't rip your Goddamn head off."

Seriousman didn't say anything at first.

But he turned around to face me, his cold blue eyes meeting my burning neon red ones.

He took a combat stance, and waved me on.

I rushed him, with Zealot calling, "Kevin, STOP!" I ignored him, and swung right handed at Seriousman. He dodged me, and dashed at Z, who drew his pistol by then and unloaded several shots into Seriousman's chest.

The crazed Superhero slammed Zealot into the wall, hard enough to knock him out, and he dropped Z on the ground. I whipped around, seeing Z on the floor and covered in blood.

Fuck, he took out the bomb defusing expert. I was too burned out on my FOCUS power to try and grab Craig from downstairs.

Seriousman turned around, and I saw three bullet holes in his chest. While he was tired, stripped of most of his powers due to Faridian exposure, and seriously wounded, Seriousman wasn't done yet. He came at me, swinging with all his might.

Putting everything Zealot taught me to good use, I dodged and weaved, punching, kicking, and beating the shit out of him as best I could.

I drove him towards the far windows, beating him senseless. When he was several feet from the tower window, I took a step back, admiring the woozy and barely standing Seriousman.

He grimaced, and grabbed me in my moment of vulnerability, tossing me at the window behind him, causing the panel to crack and spiderweb.

I glared at him, then I realized he was charging up another laser. But this one seemed much more… POWERFUL? I could hardly believe he had the will to fight through the draining of the Faridian to get his power to this level.

He hollered at me before casting his arms forward, "It's over, Villain! Die like the scum you are!"

There was no dodging or Focusing here. I was gonna have to tank this one.

I braced my legs against the floor, and crossed my arms in front of me, as Seriousman fired the biggest Hyper Beam attack he'd ever summoned at me.

The roar of twenty thousand storms erupted from his hands, with the heat of a supernova and the light of the brightest source of light you could think of, I was struck with this intense beam of energy.

I closed my eyes to the brightness, the heat searing my clothes, my skin, everything. It felt like seconds lasted for minutes. But in those seconds, my body managed to quickly adapt to the damage it was sustaining.

Even though I was experiencing heat and energy beyond anything I'd ever dealt with before, my Faridian adaptation and regeneration pulled through for me and let me endure the force of the laser. Hell, I was even able to open my eyes a bit to find out my ARM was absorbing a big amount of the energy Soups was dispelling.

I managed to begin advancing.

However, it was at that moment Seriousman ran out of power, and collapsed on the floor. He breathed heavily, and stared at me in disbelief. I shrugged my shoulders and twisted my head, popping my neck.

I walked up to him.

I clenched my left hand's fingers into a tight fist, drawing my arm back and twisting my wrist a little.

A loud whirring was heard as the compression vacuum my scientists made for my arm activated, sucking in gallon after gallon of air.

I stared Seriousman in the face as he tried stepping back away from me, but the suction the vacuum was producing was only drawing him closer.

Eventually, the vacuum stopped.

I grinned and winked at Seriousman.

I stepped forward, grabbed his head by the hair, and slammed my fist forward into his chest.

With a sonic boom, all the air my arm accumulated was released into Seriousman's body at once. Everything from the neck down was turned into a fine red mist, and his arms went out the windows at high speeds, along with shattered bones. Speaking of the windows, every single one of them shattered, all blasting outwards in a light rain of glass fragments.

I held the former Superhero's head aloft triumphantly. Then I remembered the bomb.

I ran to the bomb, which moved a little from the sonic air blast. So either Seriousman's body absorbed most of the shock, or this thing was really heavy. I dropped Soups' head and I looked all over the bomb for a panel to rip off, and I thank whatever God that was listening that I did find it. I tore it off, the sheet metal more like paper to me.

I had only 3 minutes.

I searched frantically through the wires, trying to figure out how to disarm this complicated weapon of mass destruction.

Come on Kevin, THINK!

How did Blastocyst design this fucking thing again?

I racked my brain for an answer.

When it hit me.

"Cut the power!!!"

The note Shep had in his pocket. It was how to disarm the bomb. I was so fucking blind.

I searched for another minute, and eventually found the power source, a big black box with a battery symbol on it. Saying screw it to any formality, I ripped the battery right out of the bomb.

I held my breath.

Nothing happened.

I looked at the clock.

It was off.

I heard one electronic voice speak aloud.

"Bomb detonation aborted."

I looked at the ceiling and let out a groan of relief.

I threw the battery aside and grabbed Seriousman's head, walking over to Zealot and tapping him on the head with my mechanical arm.

He stirred and rolled over to face me, only to look down at the head I had.

He looked back up to me and said, "Seriously? You ripped off his head?"

I smiled and shook the severed head, blood dripping out of it, "I keep my promises Z, you know that. Besides, won't it be freakin cool to have this mounted on the wall back home?"

He raised his eyebrows at me, "That's the first time I've heard you refrain from cursing in excess Kevin. If I didn't know you better, I'd think you might have changed throughout the course of our crusade."

My smile turned sad, as I spoke softly with a tear welling up in my eye at the memory of a good man who did good work for a bad person. "Oh, I've changed... more than you could know..."

He then pushed himself to his feet, glaring at me as he said, "You're not taking that home with you. It's staying here."

I whined and complained about it on the ride all the way down the elevator.

* * * * *

The elevator took less time than I expected. It felt like we were in there for no more than a minute before the metal box dinged on our floor and the doors slid open on the ground level. I walked out, my feet clanging against the marble tile floor, and I was greeted to the sight of an all too familiar SWAT team lined up outside the front.

A similarly familiar female voice called out to the building in an annoyed, demanding tone, "Just lay down your weapons, if you have any, and come out with your arms raised above your heads, and we will take you into custody without any harm to you. Don't act like nobody is in there, I can clearly see you hiding behind the pillars and the plants, you aren't that sneaky!"

I trudged down the stairs, with Z close behind, and I went up to Trevor who was scoping out the police, asking him, "So, I'm guessing she wants us to surrender quietly?"

Trev grunted in confirmation, adjusting his scope zoom, "Yeah, she's got the whole place surrounded. We aren't getting out of this one scot free boss, I hate to admit it."

I patted him on the shoulder, and walked for the front doors. Zealot followed me, however he stopped me by them, getting my attention before addressing me.

"Kevin, before we go out there, I want to ask you something..."

I raised an eyebrow at him, and rested my hands in my pockets, prompting him with, "Ask away buddy."

He looked outside for a moment, and seemed to hesitate with his next question, "Do you want me to join you out there, or do you want me to stay here with the others?"

At first, I didn't understand why he was volunteering to stay behind. But after studying his face for a moment, I go the memo. He didn't want me to suffer another loss like when Shepard was killed. He wanted his inclusion to be a conscious decision, not one made out of habit or a feeling of obligation towards my second in command.

I looked out toward the barricade of SWAT members, at the leader at the front, biting my lip in calculation. This lady, whoever she was, knew me already. Staring her down at the museum saw to that. She was likely a Hero of her own kind, an ordinary person with extraordinary skills and influence. She wasn't Super, she was human, and only that.

Maybe I could appeal to that sense of humanity?

No, who am I kidding? I was no diplomat.

Then again, that's why Zealot is here. I looked at my best friend, and nodded, giving him the thumbs up, "I'm gonna need you to talk her down for me buddy. You're Commander fuckin' Zealot, she has got to take you seriously."

He looked at me, studying my face for a moment. He then pushed open the door, and we went forward to talk our way out of the hole we dug for ourselves.

Luckily, I brought shovels and a bunch of body bags.

Side by side, Z and I walked toward the leader, with my second in command walking stiffly and with purpose, me walking like my legs were made of— ohhhh.

We stopped several yards away from the SWAT team leader, and we all stared each other down like we were in a Mexican standoff. Except this standoff was 2 against 25 or so.

So yeah it wasn't looking good.

The lady spoke through her megaphone again, "Well well well, if it isn't the resident machine man. And who's this? Dishonorably discharged veteran? Perhaps he's a friend of Commando Steve?"

Zealot narrowed his eyes, and stated to her calmly, "Put the megaphone down, and let's talk, Sarah."

I have no idea how Z knew her name, but the woman was shook. She turned off the amplifier and talked to us normally, "What did you two do this time? Has Seriousman unarmed the nuke? I would imagine so, considering how we aren't all dead."

I rolled my eyes, and said to her venomously, "Seriousman WAS the nuke, bitch. If it weren't for our intervention, this whole damn city would be a crater of ash and dirt. And YOU would be a part of those ashes."

The lady wasn't having any of it. She walked up to me and jabbed me in the chest with her finger and said, "Now listen here you megalomaniacal little shit, I don't know who you think you are—"

Zealot got between us, shoving us apart with surprising force. His eyes had that no nonsense look in them that really made me respect my right hand commander. He said, slowly and in a disgruntled manner, "Don't. Fight. Seriousman almost won. If Kevin had not acted to save us all, Seriousman would have gotten away with mass destruction on a scale no man should be allowed to get away with. You all owe Kevin your damn lives."

I raised my eyebrow at Z, and responded with, "What? Nobody owes me their LIVES, Zealot. But they DO owe me respect." I went back to glaring at Sarah.

Sarah on the other hand, looked at Z in disbelief. She looked back and forth between me and him, trying to figure out if we were serious or not.

She eventually said, "So, Seriousman was really trying to destroy the city...? But why? I don't understand..."

I shrugged, coming up empty handed with an explanation. I gave my theory to her though, as I felt she deserved that much.

"I think he just kind of felt he was out of options. He couldn't go around and just murder every Villain in Megatropolis, he was more than capable of doing it, believe me, but if he did, it would reflect on him and make him seem like a crazy and out of control vigilante like

Commando Steve. So he had to find roundabout ways of having them die, probably via accidents of some sort, but if a bunch of accidents coincidentally occurred with him present, it would seem extremely suspicious and he would be investigated.

"So he eventually came to the conclusion he would need to kill all the Villains at once, and in a way so catastrophic that it would anger the public and bring them to call for the destruction of the Villains as a whole, and effectively untie his hands. What weapon does catastrophic damage and levels a city? A nuclear weapon.

"But if he used a real nuke, that could result in civilians suffering the consequences, so he needed a clean nuclear option. So he went to Professor Blastocyst and got the plans for the doctor's most powerful bomb that would basically atomize Megatropolis with no harmful side effects like radioactive fallout."

I took a deep breath after that long winded exposition dump.

Sarah bit her lip, considering what I was just telling her. She took a moment, before asking me, "So, who else could have known about Seriousman's plan?"

I listed off a few people off the top of my head to her, "Harbiter, who was basically his best friend, Commando Steve, who he was probably going to blame for the destruction of Megatropolis since he got the crazed man on his side, the mayor, who likely just turned the other way…"

I swear I saw Sarah's eyes light up in anger, as bright and as red as mine. But she shook her head, and her eyes were back to an amber. She nodded and said curtly, "Okay. I…" she forced the next thing she said through her teeth, "THANK YOU for saving our city, Kevin."

And with that, she turned and walked away, waving at her men to stand down and move out.

Huh. I guess everyone grew as people in the time it took to get here.

I turned to Zealot, my best friend, my most trusted advisor, and said with finality, "So, you know of any good homes in the suburban area near your place?"

He turned for the building and started walking, throwing behind him, "I already found a place you'll love Kev."

I ran after him, wondering if Steve had made it down the stairs by now, or if I was going to have to carry him down.

Maybe we could drop him from the top of the stairwell, it would take less time and we could get lunch after. >~<

What did I tell you about making that face.

Fuck off, nobody asked you.

Epilogue: The Man Who Saved The City

News spreads like wildfire in this city.

When everyone found out Seriousman was in fact the man who would have destroyed the city if not for my intervention, many were devastated, and many more called for the removal of the mayor (the man who enabled such a corrupt figure in the first place), in favor of me being put in power instead.

I was an overnight celebrity.

"The Guardian Angel of Megatropolis" they called me. Pfft. As if I had wings or something. Anyways, me and my crew were heralded as the new greatest Heroes of the city, replacing the corrupt and lawful evil bastards who were once Superheroes.

In my many months of being mayor I cleaned the whole city up, top to bottom. I hunted down Villains and Heroes alike, giving no quarter to Superhumans who would dare stand in my way.

My Faridian arm proved to be almost overpowered, negating all their powers and killing them with enough exposure.

I was effectively a god among mankind. The exception, however, was Steve.

Steve went into hiding, and I never caught sight nor sound of the sneaky bastard since that fateful day in the tower.

But I felt like there was more to my success than just me being powerful and a badass.

That's because, obviously, there was.

Zealot was invaluable in my campaign. He made me more popular than the President of the United States at the time. I was known throughout the country as the greatest Superhuman alive.

With time, people lobbied for me becoming President.

And by Jove, this was apparently such a huge movement, I was in the campaign running for my first term, with Zealot as my Vice President.

The polls came in, eventually.

Zealot walked into my house one day (I got my own place after taking Megatropolis), walked into my kitchen where I was enjoying some cheesecake, and he threw an envelope at me, saying with a slight half smile, "Congratulations, mister President."

I did laps around the whole fuckin city after that news.

And with that, I guess I'll stop. I mean, what else is there left to talk about? I've spent several hours talking into this speech to text app, and my throat hurts a little.

I'm the President of the United States now. And while nobody else really believes me, I have a feeling people are gonna try to pull me out of power soon here.

I'm having Z make sure that doesn't happen. I'll be more than President soon enough. I'll be the King of the USA.

And after that, the world will be mine.

Even if I have to fight everyone on the planet to do so.

For now, this is the World's Greatest Supervillain, Kevin Andréson, and I'm heading out to visit my… former best friend, and where he… rests for eternity.

. . . .

May you rest in peace, buddy chum pal.